Georgia Carys Williams was born in Swansea. She won third prize at the Terry Hetherington Award 2012, highly commended for The South Wales Short Story Competition 2012, was shortlisted for the Swansea Life Young Writing Category of the Dylan Thomas Prize, 2008 and for the Wells Festival of Literature 2009. Whilst working on a PhD in Creative Writing at Swansea University, she writes for *Wales Arts Review* and was commissioned by the Rhys Davies Trust to contribute to *WAR*'s fictional map of Wales series. Most recently, she was shortlisted for *New Welsh Review*'s Flash in the Pen competition, published in Parthian's *Rarebit* Anthology and awarded third prize in the Terry Hetherington Award 2014.

www.georgiacaryswilliams.com
@veryeglantine

D1461808

Second-hand Rain

Second-hand Rain

Georgia Carys Williams

Parthian
The Old Surgery
Napier Street
Cardigan
SA43 1ED

www.parthianbooks.com

First published in 2014
© Georgia Carys Williams 2014
All Rights Reserved

ISBN 978-1-909844-84-1

Editor: Susie Wild
Cover design by theundercard.co.uk
Front cover image: Dana Duncan, flickr.com/photos/buzzygirl/
Typeset by Elaine Sharples
Printed and bound by Lightning Source

Published with the financial support of the Welsh Books
Council

For Mam and Dad

'Death? Why this fuss about death? Use your imagination, try to visualize a world *without* death! [...] Death is the essential condition to life, not an evil.'

— Charlotte Perkins Gilman

Contents

Beautifully Greek 1

Lyrebird Lament 9

Pushing Bubbles 15

Swansea Malady 27

Lady Venetia 35

Black and Yellow 49

Searching for the Fog 55

Tangerines 61

Diary of a Waste Land 71

Turnstones 83

Confidence Class 89

Nostalgia 95

My Sister, the Conductor 107

The Bereaved 119

The Girl in the Painting 131

Belongings 145

Acknowledgements 147

Beautifully Greek

My knees hurt. I've crawled for a very long time but Mummy won't pick me up. I sometimes rest in the hallway, just to catch my breath, and then I continue to crawl towards the living room armchair where she sits. I want to be able to walk like Mummy sometimes does but I can't make it by myself without falling straight back down again. I don't know why she won't hold my hands like she used to; maybe she doesn't want me to grow any bigger.

She looks much older now; her roots have grown badger-like in their white tint and crow's feet step in and out of the corners of her eyes as they blink at the book on her lap; she doesn't turn any pages. I don't know how she expects me to see the pictures when I'm sitting all the way down here; or hear her, when she doesn't say anything out loud. If I know Mummy, she'll soon slam the story shut and start another because that one isn't colourful at all. Then, maybe I'll stretch my arms open as wide as I can until she gives me a smile.

Unlike Mummy, I've maintained my bloom of youth. My romper suit is wearing thin after twenty-three years but fits as snugly as before, and my hair, which she always said was the shade of biscuits, remains three inches long with a marvellous shine. On paper, I was named *Pseu-do-cy-e-sis*, which is difficult to pronounce, so Mummy always called me Baby, and if anyone used my official name, she'd cover my ears, then whisper straight afterwards how 'beautifully Greek' it was. As far as I could see, there was no Greek in our family and as far as the family could see, there was no *me*.

That's why they called me 'unbelievable'; unwrapped my shawl as I laid in Mummy's arms, then allowed its silk corner to recoil and steal my breath away. After that, Mummy cuddled me closer and promised she wouldn't let them visit us again.

My earliest memory is of me and Mummy being sick; just sometimes, when we woke up during dark mornings. Then she became plump, which Dad said was my fault because I enjoy jellybeans so much. He used to rush out in the middle of the night to buy pounds and pounds of them, then laugh at us both gorging on them, especially the blue ones. Just a few weeks later, we visited the doctor, which made my stomach flutter but Mummy was smiling so much as we entered the special, square room with the dim light. She said she couldn't believe it; I'd finally, after all these years, come true. The doctor said tests still had to be done.

When the phone rang at home a few days later, everything became dimmer as though we were back at the doctor's office. Mummy was so excited that she accidentally dropped the telephone after answering, so it swung like a slinky beside my ear and there was the doctor's voice echoing through Mummy's tummy, to me.

'We've received the results, and they were negative.' I could feel Mummy's heart racing above me, which made mine race after it. 'Hello? Hello? Are you still there?'

I tried to speak back but nothing came out, and the next moment, Mummy was slamming the phone down so hard that it made me jump.

'They can't be sure of anything yet; not while you're the size of a jellybean!'

That same day, Mummy told Dad he should begin to call me 'Baby' but he wouldn't. Instead, he acted as though I wasn't there, so I kicked him once when they were making love, entwined together like sugared, liquorice laces, but it was just to catch his attention. Then I watched him pause and lose interest in his actions for a while before he yanked the blankets over them and continued. He found it more difficult to ignore me on the next occasion, and the occasions after that. Yes, that must have been it because he didn't get that close to either of us again, not for months. Mummy seemed sad about it.

A couple of months later, Dad sent us to another square room for psychotherapy. All we had to do was talk, which Mummy had no problem with; she always chatted to me. What she did have a problem with was the therapist saying my real name so many times and so quickly that there was nothing Mummy could do about it.

'Now, you had the ultrasound again a few days ago and as I'm aware you've already discussed with your GP, there was no sign of foetal tissue, so we've established this as a case of *Pseu-do-cy-e-sis,*' she said, 'which you have to believe. That's the first step towards you getting better! Also, there's more chance of you conceiving if you're feeling less stressed.'

I could see that Mummy wasn't listening, and I was confused: I remembered tumbling around as much as I could under Mummy's tummy when they spread that jelly all over my back. 'But I don't need to conceive,' she said, 'my periods stopped *weeks* ago and my breasts feels so tender. I'm telling you, all the symptoms are here! You only have to look at me to see!' Then she pointed right at me. I wanted to mention being thirsty all the time but the therapist was always interrupting me.

'It's all in the mind, I'm afraid. I know it's extremely difficult to understand but what you're currently experiencing is gaseous distension of the bowel.' I was glad *that* didn't turn out to be my name; it's nowhere near as beautiful.

Mummy was offered pills another time, to prevent the 'cessation of menstruation' but Mummy defended me. She said swallowing them would be like aborting her perfectly healthy child. I still *am* perfectly healthy.

3

'This is a false pregnancy,' the GP said. 'I can't stress how important it is for you to remember this baby does not exist.'

That's when we left the room. Mummy wouldn't stay unless the doctor believed we were both there.

I even remember the labour. Just before it, was 'Braxton Hicks', a name I wouldn't have minded so much, but during my birthday, there was lots of disappointment. Dad was there and he looked sad holding Mummy's hand, telling her it would all be over soon – and it was, but that didn't mean it wasn't difficult for us both; they were quite rough with me and kept calling me 'a shame', 'Isn't it a shame?' they asked, and I wanted to spit out that I was a baby.

It was a home birth because I wasn't allowed a bed at the hospital where there were going to be other, 'real' babies. I tried to make myself stand out; rolling and tumbling and crossing my legs over each other as I fought my way through, but 'labour without delivery' was what they called it in the end, at the precise moment I saw Dad's hands were held open, ready to catch me.

'He has no weight,' Dad said, and Mummy sneered at him, her face as pink as mine, our wet strands of hair flopping onto our foreheads. 'It's as if he isn't even here,' Dad added, causing Mummy to cry even louder than me, but I was there, there's no doubt about that; I remember how grainy his hands were as I wriggled in them, the roughest thing I've ever felt other than this carpet. I like to think Mummy's cries were substitutes for what Dad was adamant not to hear.

'I understand it must be awful for you to believe you're bearing a child and then discover quite the opposite,' another doctor said to Mummy weeks later. I was used to the dim light by now. 'It might take a while for the shape to disappear entirely,' he said, and I wondered where I'd gone. I didn't want to leave but I was worried Dad was going to send me away and that was why Mummy had been holding the blanket so tightly around me

4

before placing me in the nursery cot. She would sit alongside me for hours, quietly singing lullabies. Then one night, as my eyes were about to close, I saw hers become a teary glaze. 'Phantom baby, *phantom*! They think you're just imaginary, can you believe it?' she was muttering to me: 'As if you're not a baby,' she said, 'but something *else*.' Then, telling me not to be frightened, she smoothed the frown from between my eyes. I couldn't help feeling concerned; I worry a lot.

Mummy could see me for a while after the birth. She never forgot to kiss my forehead before we woke up together and always fed me her milk before rocking me back to sleep.

'You're not mad, Mummy,' I used to say. At the time, I couldn't pronounce my words very well but she'd smile back at me, whispering comfort. We always understand each other. Dad, on the other hand, kept saying how ridiculous it was, having a nursery for an invisible child and an intercom that heard nothing but the buzzing of its own on-switch. After that, I began to see myself in the mirror.

Dad didn't like me; I'm not sure he does now. He never held me and always avoided eye contact, and yet once, I heard him mutter something in the nursery, just before he cleared it out and refurbished it to be a study. He just stood there, in the centre of the room, staring at the cot and the bears surrounding me as I rose onto my toes and clung to the wooden bars. I'd learn to keep things tidy, I wanted to say. Really, I would; I'd be the tidiest baby around, but he sighed, 'Ah, we wanted you so much,' which I did believe, but Dad didn't realise that with no place for me to sleep, I had to lie between him and Mummy every night, growing a little as the weeks went on.

It wasn't long before the milk dried up and I felt myself being held in Mummy's arms, which seemed more limp than usual. Still, I clung on as tightly as I could, with my mouth open wide.

'Mummy, can you not see me?' I kept asking.

'Mummy, can you not see me?'

But I think she only saw me in glimpses: when I learnt to sit up, when I learnt to crawl. That teary glaze must have altered her vision. I still can't walk, but I learnt to talk just by listening to Mummy. I used to scream, but it had no effect. Sometimes I hold her hand, but she flinches. It's difficult to comprehend; that space I took up when I was swelling up like a bowling ball in her stomach. That *weight* is in the space around her and yet she can ignore it so easily now. She ignores me as I crawl after her, grasping onto her stubbly ankles and hanging like a dead weight. What does it mean when my tummy growls at me?

I see other children sometimes. They tell me they have the same name, '*Pseudocyesis*', so I tell them how beautiful it is, how Greek it is and they smile. They don't have Mummies. We have learnt to be the children watching life and not playing a part. Sometimes I notice Mummy staring longingly at other toddlers in pushchairs and I feel jealous, I begin to hate them. Perhaps someday, Mummy will find me; surely she can't forget. I can see her when she smiles false smiles and I wish people would notice as I do, saying 'False! Unbelievable,' but I heard her talk about me after a few years had passed. It was when a lady walked past in the street and she asked how I was.

'Oh, it's a long story,' Mummy mumbled, as though I wasn't a child, but something *else*. So I feel a little betrayed. I'm a much taller story now. 'Don't be frightened, Baby,' she had told me all that time ago, yet I think she's quite frightened of herself. I'm scared she'll never call me Baby again.

Pseu-do-cy-e-sis. My paper-name is difficult to pronounce all by myself. *Pseudocyesis?* Is that all it is? I'm determined to learn as much as I can from Mummy. She knows a lot. She sees the world more openly than other people and the three of us have visited lots of places together since the beginning. She should know I'm only as old as she allows me to be but she's not letting me grow;

maybe she really doesn't want me to get any bigger. Sometimes, I still try to lie between her and Dad, like the child they had always wanted, but neither seem comfortable with it anymore, not even Mummy; perhaps because I am older now, perhaps because I am twenty-three.

They've both retired now, but I don't see them in the same room very often. When I do, I don't hear them saying anything, not even about me, so I'm beginning to forget what their voices sound like. Mummy's used to sound like whispers. I hope they're not silent because I'm singing so loudly, but I want to show I remember the songs Mummy taught me because I don't want them to forget how much I need to be looked after.

Most days, I crawl back and forth between the living room and the kitchen, then up and down the stairs with all the strength I can muster to lift each leg, but my knees, they hurt. I go wherever Mummy's warmth goes, wherever that smell, sweet like jellybeans, goes, which I remember from the times she used to hold me against her chest and gently rub my back. It made me dozy with its deep sound, *ba-boom, ba-boom, ba-boom*. Sometimes, I fall asleep in the hallway, just thinking about it; sometimes for days.

I can't help yawning now. The carpet makes my knees sore and my hands are bright red, look! I'm trying my best to stand without holding onto anything but I can't, so I'm reaching out with my arms, trying to keep my balance, and smiling at Mummy at the same time. Oh, she's sitting up. Now she's added her book to the pile on the coffee table, but why isn't she looking at me? I'm standing right here.

'Mummy! I'm right here.'

Doesn't she care to pick me up? Why doesn't she want to cuddle me? My knees, they hurt. I want Mummy to kiss them better.

Lyrebird Lament

I am the laugh of a kookaburra. I am a currawong. I am a galah. I am a lyre because I am a lyrebird. I am a performer and I am superb.

I've performed every winter of my life in the lush, green forest. I was born into the drama, into the bellowing music of males I looked up to, or down on, depending on my position on a nearby tree. They were inspirational from the start, with their feathery tails fanned over their heads like stage curtains, almost tribal in their side-to-side and circling footsteps. They looked alive. That's how I learnt so much, by observing, by remembering and recording: seeing their fifty-minute shows provided me with entertainment, but also something to look forward to, something to achieve. I was told I would have the chance to sing out like the others, eventually. 'At the moment, you're just a plain-tail,' they said.

Competition was always drilled into me. I knew I needed to have a good memory but also be a good listener, which meant a high level of self-interest was impossible. I needed to remember everything so accurately to impersonate it properly. 'Practice makes perfect,' was another thing they said, and was mainly what my life consisted of: I am this, I am that. From the trees, it all looked so easy initially, but I couldn't have been more wrong. It took great concentration to get it right and when it happened, I felt elated. Other than the *choo choo* of my own voice, I sounded my first call, which was the laugh of a kookaburra. I was attempting it over and over again *oo oo oo oo oo OO, oo oo oo oo oo oo*

OO, oo oo oo oo oo OO, ahahaha. Then I heard the sound, exactly the same as the one I'd made. Whether it was another lyrebird or not, I couldn't be sure, but I knew it was the feeling of success. I did it again and heard it again and then I was addicted; over and over I was chuckling and always looking for the next sound.

From that moment on, I truly became myself, which I discovered was a *lot* of different things, but 'one note wrong,' the elders said, and the audience could end up on someone else's side, and who was the audience? They were the plainer birds, brown like pheasants and never quite as noisy as the rest of us, but that didn't matter, I knew I liked them, females were the prize. When I was younger, I used to forage along the forest floor in the company of other young males and females; we used to rake up leaves and soil to find earthworms and search rotting logs for insects and beetles. My interests changed when I was about three years old because even though my feathers had been falling away every year, they'd grown back longer each time. At that point, with my fully-formed lyre-tail, I was prepared to work alone. I could finally perform.

I began building mounds for the show and when I was ready and the weather was right, I would race up to one of them as fast I could and begin performing straightaway. I began with the *choo choo* to draw attention to myself and when I saw the blemishes of brown appearing in the distance, I would really show off, first with the kookaburra and next, the squeak of the currawong along with anything else I'd learnt. *I am I am I am* would whirl around in my head as I'd synchronise the sounds, such a colourful carnival of voices. Then I'd run to the second mound, then the third. I would walk backwards, then forwards, then backwards, and then spin around, rotating my veil of feathers.

I loved the sense of it all, you know, the atmosphere. For about fifty minutes, I would stand and perform with my ferny fringe fanning over my face, then tap my feet, seeing the excitement in

10

their eyes, all because they were watching me. There was a sense of achievement in being able to finally display what I'd tried so hard to learn for so many years. That moment gave me confidence.

'I can be anything,' I told myself. It was clear that I could.

After that, my songs became more and more elaborate. It was a show that was only cancelled by the rain, which could ruin my lacy feathers and any future performances. I even chased other males out of my territory if I thought they'd threaten my success, my fame, my living to excess. At the end of the spinning, my head and wings would begin to shiver from left to right so fast: they must have looked like a blur, vibrating as though they were shaking something away. Then I'd start making a clicking sound until I'd impressed at least three of the females. Then I'd stop, standing still before the next scene, which was the most interesting to the birds in the trees. It involved only two of us: me and another female. Then the show would be over until next time.

As time went on, I began to hear different noises in the forest, more unsettling ones. There was one in particular, a sort of buzz that went *vrrr, vrrrr, VRRRRRR* or *whoa whoa WHOA* with the background of a crackly *zzzzzzz*. I spent as much time trying to ignore it as I did paying attention to it. It was quite difficult to mimic because its grumble seemed to fluctuate. I tried to warn it away by singing one of my most melodious tunes, which lasted a long time but I had to let them know, this was *my* home.

As I said, it was rare for performances to be cancelled. Everyone had always been so eager and it wasn't raining, so I didn't understand why no one was rushing to my show. The sounds of other birds seemed so far away. While I was resting amongst the trees, I heard that sound again. *Vrrrr vrrrr, zzzzzzzzzzzz,* but it sounded a lot closer than before. I considered how this could be the perfect chance to learn it properly, to possess it, just as I had with every other sound in the past. I managed to find a branch in the distance, from which I could see where the sound was coming from, *Zzzzzzzzzzz*, and then I spotted something moving. I jumped down and ran as fast as I could across the forest floor towards it. It wasn't a bird, that I was sure of. It was a human holding something sharp, with huge, serrated teeth and it was cutting away at the forest. I watched, seeing tree after tree tumble down, causing the ground to tremble beneath me. I felt sorry for the creatures over there; they must have been terrified.

Days afterwards, I became ill. My eyes and nostrils became runny and I couldn't breathe very well; I felt like there was some kind of dust trapped in my throat. I wanted to warn the other lyrebirds about what I'd seen but competition meant I'd chased them all away a long time ago, aggressively charged at them, so I probably wouldn't see anyone anytime soon. I didn't know whether it was the delirium of my illness, but I was sure that sound was moving closer. Everything sounds loud when you're drifting off to sleep, but this was an unbearable noise.

One morning, it was all made clear. It was closer, very close indeed. It was a human holding a chainsaw and it was ready to cut down the tree I'd roosted in the night before. When I heard its *zzZzZzz* not yet upon the bark, I quickly jumped down from the log I was perched upon, then raced across the forest floor again, but it seemed there were trees being amputated before me and as they fell, the pounding caused me to be thrown against a log, which was where I stayed. Just across from me, I could see one of those plainer females lying on her side, a small branch across her tail feathers; that's why she hadn't come to watch me. I wondered about other birds perched high up in the branches and I hoped they'd escaped. I tried to shriek as a warning but nothing emerged from my beak. I tried to imitate what I'd been practising in recent weeks, that same *ZzZzzzzZzz* but nothing sounded other than a raspy crackle and panting breath. I'd lost my voice.

I can't be sure exactly where I was discovered but I remember waking up with at least three humans standing around me. I felt nervous but their faces weren't as menacing after they'd laid the chainsaws down.

'This one's alive. We'll send him to Adelaide Zoo. He'll put on a good show,' said one of them. That was the first mention of another show I'd heard in a long time, so at that moment, I felt excited, even when I spotted the trunks of my old home making their way out of the forest on an eight-wheeled truck.

'They'll have to get him better first, mate,' another voice said, the sound too complex for me to even contemplate imitating for a long time. 'He's a skinny thing. Shouldn't be that small. Looks like some sort of flu.' I was lucky to be alive. Then I was placed in a box on the back of a different truck altogether and sent away to the new show. It must have been the nerves that caused me to vomit all over my face. I fell asleep breathing in the rich smell through my already stuffed-up nostrils.

I'm at the zoo now, in Adelaide, where I often daydream about my old home. I see the colours, hear the sounds and imagine running and running and running, chasing off all competition. I'd sing all day, marking out my territory, but now I wake up, dancing in circles, before crashing into the fencing that marks it. Gazing through the mesh, home always seems so far away that I wonder if I've imagined it all, even the males from whom I learnt my performances. I used to perch low in a tree and watch them, didn't I? As soon as I approach this detail, my daydream always turns into a nightmare, with chainsaws that devour the trees. Sometimes I still hear their growl, *zzzZZZZzzz, ZZZzzzzz*, louder and louder.

I haven't noticed as many female birds either. They don't seem to be around here, no matter how much I sing, dance or run around. I miss their plainness, their brown dullness; they're the audience I want. They used to make me feel better about myself;

I was always a winner, but now, I reap no rewards. Sometimes, I put on a display and no one comes to watch at all. Whose side are my audience on now?

I regained my health after the zoo took me in. They do take care of me; I feel safe, which of course I'm grateful for, but even when my ability to make sounds returned, I'd lost all my previous identities: I can't laugh like a kookaburra; I definitely can't laugh, I need to practise but I can't quite hear the sound. Instead, I cry the cry of a human baby. I've learnt every one of a writer's words: he visits and sits alongside my fence each week and reads my story aloud as though he's me, as though he's stealing my identity. I have an audience I don't want.

Now, I am the horn of a railway. I am a lumberjack. I am a car alarm. I am the shot of a rifle. I am a dog barking. I am a human voice. I am a camera. I am a lyre because I am a lyrebird. I am a performer and I am superb.

Pushing Bubbles

My mother thought it would be perfect for a Piscean to be born in bath water, gasping for air like an un-gilled fish. She imagined it as a dive from womb to womb, or an early baptism, but she wasn't religious. She said, if the water could hold me, she'd trust that she could too. Dad said he scooped me out before I could cry.

There was a time when Dad considered my mother's fear of hurting me to be ridiculous. That was before he witnessed me at three years old, bubble-covered and tiptoeing over the bathroom windowsill, held out like a sacrificial lamb.

'She's never seen snow,' my mother was saying, and I remember that part clearly, probably because it was true. Even though she'd created this scene from soap and water, the thousands of pearlescent swirls and fizz were the most beautiful thing I'd ever seen. She was pushing them out of the window and letting them fall softly to the lawn. *Look at that,* I remember her saying, *look at that,* as her long, ice cold hands made sure my head stayed turned towards the sky and the metal of her rings dug into my cheeks. I remember waiting for something to happen, but bubbles make no sound, if I recall, apart from a slight crackle, and when they disappear into the grass, nothing at all.

From bathwater, the earth felt upside down. I was on my back, my bare bottom-half suspended as my toes rested upon the frosty taps. I saw their reflection of me: three, grey, elongated heads faltering around the Jacuzzi jets pocked into the ceramic. It was only my head weighing me down. Dad had told me a long time ago not to bother using the bath, especially when I was alone in the house, but since I was fifteen and it was the Christmas holidays, I assumed that rule had expired.

For many minutes, I was lulled back and forth, allowing my feet to climb the long neck of the shower and my face to dip beneath the surface. It made me feel like a capsized canoe, or with my eyes shut, a bat, using sound to see. As I held my breath underneath, I heard my own heartbeat but it was out of time with the jets. I tried to keep up with the rhythm, but I couldn't, so I rose and returned to rocking, seeing the pointed silk of my hair levitating around my shoulders and strumming at the water. Its long elegance unexpectedly reminded me of my mother.

Over the years, my mother, in her absent way, had become an elaborate character of my imagination, a goddess figure 'too good for this world', as some would say of the dead; too tender, with a distant look in her eyes as though she was gazing towards the place where she was supposed to be. Nature trapped in a human body was how I thought of her, a fast-growing tree with branches so long, they couldn't help but curl back inwards until the leaves were left to pierce her skin. The woman I'd since met in Nan's living room, however, was a dull imposter, a bare outline whose nodding head stuck out when it smiled, and at the same time gave her a slight hunch, causing her blouse to fall all wrong at the shoulders.

It wasn't often that I saw this woman, and as I got older, the images I'd originally created became so static that it took more and more effort to fuel life into them. I'd read all the books my mother had left behind, so it almost felt like I'd pushed the image to its limits, used all the resources I could find for her personality, since Dad didn't talk about her as often anymore. Over time, the character grew as still as one of the living room's wall-hangings and more like the woman I met in person every April, (for her

16

birthday and never for mine), whose speech sounded like a frozen rehearsal of how-are-yous and keeping-well-thank-yous. Gradually, I forgot my past-mother ever existed.

That was until I was lying in the bathtub, imagining myself as a sinking Ophelia in the glow of the green bath light. I couldn't help thinking of how characteristic of my mother it was to do this, to magically emerge like some siren from the water at the least expected of moments, like a wave in the already bubbling current.

It was a shame when something started to cloud my experience: dark brown, rusty crisps of stagnant water like the crumble from the leaves of trees in summer were floating out of the jets and they wouldn't stop. I tried to disguise them beneath the bubbles but they caught between the white comb and soon, there were so many splinters that they crept up my arms, calves and thighs like the flakes of cremated toast or tea leaves and they were making me stew in the centre of it all. Having to step out, I saw the water trembling like a giant jelly behind me as I dried myself as fast as possible before putting on a purple dressing gown, which had until then, always hung on the back of the bathroom door. The Jacuzzi was circulating what resembled a dirty cotton field. *Voom, voom, voom, voom.*

Once I'd watched the whirlpool for long enough, I unplugged the tub and saw it spin into a frenzy as the rest of the ugly remnants disappeared, then I waited ten minutes for it all to fill up again. Once the water was sitting just beneath the taps, I pressed the Jacuzzi button and watched it stir up a second soup for me to jump into.

Dipping my toes into the water first, I was about to disrobe when the phone began to ring. At the time, it had a long, electrical purr, which I could try my best to ignore but it knew all the right pitches to press, so it was only seconds before I ran downstairs to answer it, leaving the glowing water behind. I could already hear

17

Dad in my head: *what if it was something important? What would you have done then?*

I didn't know, but as I'd assumed, it was Nan calling; she used to phone every day after school to check I'd got home okay.

'Had lunch with Mum yesterday,' she said. 'She was asking after you.'

I'd noticed how she never said 'your mum', just 'Mum', as if it was my mother's name.

'I know she'd really like to see you,' she added, 'anyway, I hope you're going to make the most of your time off!' It was easier to let her steer the conversation as she pleased. 'What would you like me to buy you for Christmas?'

Thinking of my mother and remembering her perpetual smell of lavender, I told Nan that I wanted bath soaps, just in case these evenings became a habit, (and it was a gift she didn't have to think too much about). I could hear Nan shuffling around at the other end of the line, probably picking up her newspaper.

'Well, in that case, I'll give you money, so you can buy anything you like,' she said, and I could hear her sighing the way she does when she sits down.

The last time Nan had talked to Dad, he wasn't happy for weeks afterwards, he was spilling tea, tripping over his own feet and always getting angry at himself about it. At home, he'd clean for three hours every day, and every time I offered to help, he'd just say, 'No, leave it to me.' Lately, he was nervous to be around. Sometimes, he'd seem to be struck still, his arms clenched and fidgety at his sides and his ears pricking up at every sound and movement around the house.

'We might have a visitor, soon,' Dad finally said, one morning, whilst cramming a heap of clothes into the washing machine. He'd tried to casually mumble it but he was grunting every time the door jammed and the clothes piled out again. He'd decided to sweep all surfaces clear of anything but the bare essentials: 'just

18

for a while,' he said, 'we don't want anything too valuable lying around.' I didn't understand why the place had to become so barren, even an infant should have been able to handle my books, but there Dad was, piling them into the cupboard under the stairs.

Nan always talked for a while, and every time I tried to interrupt, even if only in agreement, she'd seem to squeeze her words more tightly together, wringing out the conversation so I'd have to absorb more about my mother, if she remembered anything else. As I stayed with the phone burning against my ear, I realised that even though she'd begun to relay a lot of happy details, for some reason, I didn't feel very happy listening to them.

The centre where my mother had stayed all this time was 'not as bad as you'd think,' Nan said, but it wasn't reassuring, since what I'd always pictured had been horrific, a mint-green shoe box of a room, blinded by white lights, with a narrow, little bed squashed into the corner, clinical smell of dentist overwhelming it all at the end of a long and lonely corridor where others yelled and rocked back and forth. I've never understood how the imagination can be so specific sometimes, but unless Nan pointed out any positive attributes, that's the image that seemed to stick.

As Nan chatted, I remembered the bright light responsible for waking me up during many night-times years ago; the garden light, something Dad had fitted onto the back wall of the house at a time when he was worried about potential burglars. When the disturbance became a common occurrence and there were no break-ins, he'd put it down to cats, but over time, we realised it was evidence of my mother returning from her evening wanderings.

Some nights, she wouldn't return to their room so quickly but instead, slouch herself upon the swing-seat in the corner of the garden. Noticing the light flicker before Dad did, and still only seven years old myself, I'd wander through the patio doors that my mother had left open to the breeze and there I'd find her, rocking back and forth. I can hear it now: *squeak, squeak, squeak,* sometimes so high that I could only ever see her feet, bare and blue over the edge. Then, when she'd see me watching from across the garden, she'd begin to giggle to herself and pat the upholstery next to her, so I'd join and swing alongside.

Eventually, when my mother's head would fall back with sleep, our seat would slow down and then stop, meaning that the garden light would turn off too, leaving me in the dark next to her. At first, I was frightened, so I'd focus on the moths chasing each other around the nearest street lamp, but it's funny how different things look when you stare at them for a long time. The sky, which was originally black and startling around me, gradually became comforting, and the cat's eyes that wandered across the garden fence, felt as safe as Christmas decorations. The stars formed different shapes when I closed one eye, and I remember feeling like it was a shame that there had to be holes in a sky so beautiful, even if, as my mother had said on one occasion, it was the shape of someone fighting off the darkness with a bow and arrow.

As I watched the smoky breath both escape and return to my mother's lips, it was the only thing to keep me warm beside her. However, I knew that as the moon pulled a blanket over itself, my Dad would be noticing the cold indentation of my mother in the mattress next to him. That's when he'd come stumbling outside, his eyes puffy and lop-sided as he yawned and urged us both to come back in. I doubt her imprint ever left.

All this was filtering through my head whilst talking to Nan, who was still telling me what my mother had been eating, how she'd been sleeping, and I didn't like the way my responses were sounding so adult. After eight years of my mother gone, the sentences slipped like saliva from my mouth.

'Oh, that's good then. I'm glad she's doing well,' I said. 'She'll be back to her old self in no time.'

'Yes, she's been reading again, you know. That's always good.' Nan was definitely flicking through her newspaper now.

I remembered the mornings I used to find books sprawled out across the patio before school; some of them were so ruined by the rain that the sentences had blurred into long, single words, or the paragraphs contained large, white gaps where the words used to be.

'Just bin it,' Dad would say, through gritted teeth, not even looking at the hard cover turned soft that I'd be handing to him. Then I'd walk myself to school and wonder all day, which story had disappeared? Upon return, I'd find my mother trudging around, sulkily placing a book upon the radiator or trying to dry it with a hairdryer, cursing herself and boxing with the air. The pages always stayed curled up at the corners.

One morning, Dad and I found my mother face down in the pond, hands above her head as though bowing down to something, all the fish swimming around her. When Dad picked her up, she'd folded like a marionette in his arms, but as he carried her and she came to, I remember pearls in the corners of his eyes because her arms had begun to swing at him, not caring what they hit as he tried his best to hold onto her. When she noticed me standing there and crying as I watched him take her into the house, she cried too, her wail too similar to mine, a helpless, high-pitched whine. Dad said nothing. It wasn't long afterwards that my mother left for good, slammed the door with a bang like a gunshot.

Nan was still talking to me as though I was my mother's older sister. I used to ask for a sister when I was younger, I'd even considered how it would make things easier in the future, in a practical sense. I imagined driving sixty miles to visit my mother

21

at 'the centre', the place she was supposed to become *herself again* during the brief intervals of the year when she wasn't staying with my grandparents.

'She really seems like herself again,' Nan said.

I imagined Mum's face when she was older, sat up in a white bed. It would look similar to Nan's, with the same lack of jaw line and cheekbones, but the skin would hang even more, with deeper-set wrinkles from all the prescribed drugs she'd taken just to be able to smile.

'Well, I've got to go, love.' Nan hung up then, so all I could hear was the humming of the dial-tone. I hoped she hadn't sensed how distracted I'd become, it was always difficult to think of my mother in small doses. I could tell that Dad had found it hard in the past, too. My mother seemed to carry something heavy with her and just thinking of her meant submerging yourself. I held the handset for a while, then unstuck it from my cheek. I was too warm to have a bath, so I decided to wait a while, perhaps for a time when it would be more appreciated. Even when I replaced the handset, I could still hear the constant hum.

I decided I'd help Dad out a bit and do some of the cleaning before he got home. Perhaps he'd be more relaxed than usual; not that there was much to do. I was mostly re-aligning anything I'd moved even slightly out of place in the living room and the kitchen, I added my most recent books to the cupboard, then put the kettle on so we'd be able to talk over a cup of tea.

The kettle sounded louder than usual. It was a drone that continued even after the water had boiled. So I turned off the television but it definitely wasn't that, either. It was the unfamiliar sound of the Jacuzzi, left on, *voom, voom, voom, voom.*

I ran upstairs two at a time but as I reached the landing, I heard another *voom* sound; loud like the rev of a car engine struggling up a hill. Dad had been getting home earlier the last few days, too stressed to work, he'd said, but this was much earlier than usual. The car was already reversing up the drive, which meant I only had a minute or so to make sure everything was fine.

When I reached the bathroom, facing me was an expanding jelly of white. Bubbles had risen well over a metre above the height of the bath and the uneven, rectangular mound of them was only held aside by the wavering shower curtain. The green bath light underneath sent a sickly hue throughout that made the ever-growing bath look like the gurgling stomach of a sleeping creature and as the Jacuzzi hummed on, it erupted and a layer of its bubbly contents slid from the top.

Almost slipping on them, I fought the window open and for a few seconds, just peered out, feeling the cool air on my face. Then I thrust my arm behind me and pushed some clouds of bubbles into it. They took a while to let go of my hands and when the wind caught them, they floated in suspense until they drifted to the ground.

With two arms, I pushed heap after heap of bubbles out of the window, playing a game that involved trying to destroy them faster than the bath was producing them, and as my arms began to ache, a panic overcame me. What if I couldn't do it? Was it possible to drown in bubbles? I considered that perhaps it would be more like suffocation, and they'd find me with my face pressed against the bathroom tiles, defeated by air itself. I worked faster, telling myself it was just soap and water, but it was more difficult than you'd think – the bubbles clung on to me.

Then the humming stopped.

The silence was calming and I suddenly felt the shiver of the outside upon my skin. As I turned around, I saw, there in the bubble-arched doorway, my tall and elegant mother standing with a hand on her hip, her body as bendy as before, in a long dress slightly lighter than the sky, and there was her face above it all, as though I'd conjured it after all, with the help of memories and the trouble of a bathtub. Her right arm was the only fault of her apparition, covered in froth from having turned off the jets, but it was this arm that wrapped itself around my shoulders.

'We'll sort this out,' she said. Her voice the same high pitch as before, her *t*'s, gentle, like rain against glass.

And for some reason, I believed her. Perhaps it was the swiftness of the moments after that did it, how quickly she tore the shower head from the wall, her arm seeming to grow and grow as she rinsed away as many bubbles as she could from the bath – or perhaps it was the simple way she'd sauntered through the door, the hazel of her eyes reminding me of specks of earth as soon as I'd seen them. Nevertheless, as she held the spouting weapon in her hand, I pushed and pushed into the sky as quickly as I could, seeming to find our rhythm out there, then moving even faster as I thought of the thousands of bubbles popping, those tiny, diaphanous planets colliding into one another, then becoming nothing again.

It was when we looked at each other, then shared a shriek at the hilarity of the sodden situation that I realised how the sound of her laughter had stuck with me all those years. It ricocheted against the bathroom tiles as mischievously as ever, then trickled down the walls as smoothly as condensation, and just as before, it failed to notice Dad out of breath in the doorway.

'What's going on?' His eyes were frozen into white 'O's. 'What's going on here?'

I stood there, wearing my purple robe and an awkward smile. Noticing my mother, however, Dad said nothing more. He wrapped his arm tightly around her waist as though she too, could turn to water any second, or the face that was turning to him, so shy-smiled, could just pop in mid-air.

How quickly it all seemed to happen, that all three of us were pushing the bubbles, watching them stick together as they fell, then melted into glistening reflections of the stars upon the grass outside, the flowerpots, and the swing-seat. It was then, as I saw some of them floating along the fence, that I noticed how impossible it was to push something so soft without it finding a way to squeeze itself into every opening, then melting away so slowly that I wouldn't even realise. And yet there we stood, all of us pushing bubbles, an arm of each of my parents around me so they spread out like full-grown wings, some of our fingertips ahead of us, accidentally touching.

Swansea Malady

Its breath is the strongest, stifled by something in the pit of its stomach, green with grumble and blue with malady. It catches you, and like the fish around Mumbles pier, you can't quite let go. You open your nose to the sickly-sweet smell of seaweed and you hear the farcical shriek of gulls in the air, pining for you to look up. Then you're thrown, out of the sea and straight into rain.

I've heard people speak of water having a memory and I wonder if it's better than my grandfather's is, as I look at the sea trembling in and out of Swansea Bay like a tired hand. As I step across the quilted impression of the sand, I wonder what it's seen. Does it drift in and out in the same, slow manner, with every base of its stories strewn upon the seabed, only the shrapnel of shells to be dragged back in?

Head over shoulder as I see the prints of my toes among the pinned shells, my feet have led me to a large mound of sand; they've crept into a circular castle built at the end of the bay. Stopping to observe its structure, I'm glad I haven't done much damage other than a slight indentation in the side and although I feel the urge to sink my foot entirely into it, remembering the striped tail of apartments overlooking the dunes, I tell myself to resist. I remind myself of how it must feel for someone to build something so intricate and then witness it being reduced to rubble.

Mesmerised by the exhibit, I crouch down to its lopsided shape, which is layered to resemble a decadent birthday cake. It has

27

spindles for turrets as though it belongs to a realm of fairies and phantoms, and the only article missing is the roaring dragon of the Welsh flag on the top.

I stand up, feeling the ache in my thighs stretching out and as I drag my feet along the damp sand of the bay, I think of all that remains of the real Swansea Castle; its grey, carcassed elbow joint at the centre of town.

This is I, it would project with a gravelly voice if it could speak, like the proud, stubborn voice of my grandfather who has smoked cigars since the war. He sometimes speaks about the smoke during The Blitz and I look to the left and see the long sewage pipes stretching out into the sea like two, long arms.

As boys, we used to dive right off those, he'd say.

This morning, before attending an arts afternoon called 'Transitions', I walked through the centre of town and heard the guitar's hollow pluck of a song I recognised to be Jeff Buckley's cover of 'Hallelujah' disappearing shyly behind the murmur of Swansea Market, then ringing through town. I couldn't make out what the musician looked like but through the hoard of people, I saw a splatter of silver upon the black felt of his open guitar case. I filled in the lyrics I could remember as I walked past. Then it was the instrumental in ascending steps before it broke out, then hid again, ebbing into the market.

My grandfather said the market used to be the best in Wales; a grandiose glass-iron structure around all sorts of stalls: cafés, fishmongers, clothes, vegetable and clock stalls.

We used to love laverbread and Penclawdd cockles from the market, he'd say, *lovely with a bit of bacon fat. Sometimes, we'd have black beef or salt marsh lamb at the weekend. Over six hundred stalls, it had!*

He'd start one story and, without ending it, begin another about the picnics on the top of Kilvey Hill or The Lion's Head, and I'd feel the shrapnel of memories hitting me as his eyes looked into mine. Sometimes, he'd stop talking altogether.

There have been especially good days, where he's almost told a whole story, but I only know this because he will have certainly told it before. He asks me questions as though I'm someone else, his old friend, his brother or even my passed away grandmother. It's when things alter around him that he becomes confused; suffers from forgetfulness. At that moment, it feels just like the sand slipping through my toes.

It was at the arts afternoon that people spoke about water having a memory. There was the verbal kind of art, poetry and storytelling, the kind that can speak loudly from some place deep and there was music, yet it didn't seem to transcend as emotively as the strum of the busker's guitar I'd passed earlier on. There had been paintings, but they were too abstract for my taste, too undecided about their own motives and I was desperate to leave. More shrapnel hits me:

Without the cracks, we have nothing to fill; without the empty canvas, we have nothing to paint.

So I quickly paid my respects, then stepped out of the theatre and onto the cobble-stoned Marina where the Helwick ship was perched like a smoked-out dragon, dead on its back.

Here on the beach, I see the sand-cemented walls of the castle before me and wonder how easily I could move it. I place two arms either side of the castle's curve and close my eyes, ready to turn it over like a just-baked cake but the base doesn't budge, only the edge begins to turn to dust and fall as grain in my hands. I step back, wondering where the rest of Swansea went in my grandfather's memory. *The beach is always here,* he'd said, *it only changes shape.* I wonder where its laughter lines are, feeling the sandbanks bowing around me.

After The Blitz, Swansea's face wasn't smiling anymore. It was shattered. The sandcastle stands there so proud that I ask myself what the urge is to break something so beautiful that someone else has created. I think I'm alone, but I look up and notice a couple, their arms in a figure of eight as they walk down the slope and onto the beach:

> foreheads together
> but lips not,
> words together
> but tongues not.

My rucksack is full of glass tumblers, equipment intended for this afternoon's performance, but I didn't use them, I told the other artists I'd forgotten my material, and then hastily walked towards the door. Afraid they could hear the clinking of the hollow, glass harmonica upon my back, I didn't turn around but kept pacing away until I'd escaped the building and reached the gull-filled air, bubble-wrapped glasses behind me. I was intending to fill each with a different amount of water and hear Welsh tunes upon the glass by striking them with a wooden pencil, but it would have sounded so mediocre.

I let go of my rucksack and place it upon the sand next to me, removing the glass stack. Tumbler after tumbler, I press holes for each base to sink into, just a few metres from the tide. I save the eighth to be the water collector, scooping the sea into it before pouring it into the others, steps of memory from left, to right. Sitting cross-legged in front of them, I use a wooden pencil to try and mimic the beautiful music I'd heard on my way through town. Not much happens other than the dull ding of different tones that could be played by the hand of a child.

I glance to the left, past the imposing, charcoal wall of the harbour and towards the Marina. If I close my eyes, I'm there, in whatever moment I choose. Last time, I walked right to the end of the harbour wall, where there were newspapers foot-stepped so hard to the ground that there were some from the 1970s. My grandfather and I bought salted chips and ate them under the archways until the evening drew in, the Marina's black water growing solid beneath the reflection of its dusky, yellow lights.

Now kneeling behind my octave of glasses, sunlight glimmers through the beaded glass, clammy sand grasping onto it. I lie on my stomach and look at the sea through the smudged lenses. It rolls in and out, creeping over me like the murky sheets of a penny slot machine at the arcade and leaving remnants of white horses jumping over my flattened palms.

Then I see the blur of a girl nearing the fairytale sandcastle, her coat a bold blue, magnified in the side of one of the tumblers. Sitting up, I see that she pokes her fingers through its windows and doors, and then places them flat on each step. This castle has two levels. With less thought than I, she sits in the centre, squashing the sand so it makes the circle a little larger around her, only laughing quietly enough for herself and I to hear. She leaves as it begins to rain.

Leaving the glasses to their own devices, I draw another circle around the castle's moat, giving it more depth than before. The castle looks a little stunted but sturdy remnants of it stand tall with the foundations still laid. I trace the space of a graveyard, for all the people who used to walk there, their booming voices and the incantation of necromancers echoing from the turrets. I provide each grave with a shell for a headstone and dig elongated dips into the sand to leave room for their bodies. I look to the tide, which is moving in.

I can still hear my grandfather speaking about the same, magnificent things. *There was talk of a tunnel under the seabed, running from Swansea Castle, all the way to Oystermouth Castle!* Once again, I place my arms either side of the castle, wanting to break it before the waves reach it, but even with gapless fingers, I'm incapable. I peer into one of the sandcastle's windows, and then picture myself standing inside it.

I imagine curling up within the remains of Swansea Castle, its voice luring me towards the top of a cobblestoned Wind Street, a compact watering hole for the sober eager to topple. The corner is marked by a building with a Tudor skin, which is also a bar, and I begin to feel out of place. On this oddly warm, spring evening, I'm drawn in by the aroma of chips and hot dogged air, I see women ahead of me with empowered looks but sparse clothing, and men roaring above club music that already vomits out onto the street.

As always, I find myself at the storm-less No Sign Bar, a more subdued and authentic pub, which I've heard has a yearning for journos. I'm not one, but I prefer this portrayal of Swansea, where the live music of folk band sings up the fire exit steps from The Vault. After drinking a glass of their house wine, I remember why I'm here in this haze, so I walk back out into the air where it's still light.

I often visit Mumbles, so I've seen the green-bellied hill of Oystermouth Castle and been one of a couple holding each other's hands, afraid to wipe the white of ice cream from the corners of their mouths. *There used to be a tram from the bottom of Wind Street, which ran all the way to the end of Mumbles Pier,* says the voice of my grandfather. From here, my mind is on the tram and with each retracing, my grandfather's voice is chiming in. *I courted your grandmother in Mumbles,* he says, and as we reach the dismantled, old stone bridge, I imagine him pointing to the right. *You could hire deck chairs and take donkey rides along the beach.* His stubby fingers change direction. *Oh! The Patti Pavilion! That's where I first saw your grandmother, waltzing around the mirrored pillars. Her reflection was never as good again once she started dancing with me!* It's a restaurant now.

After a few blinks, I vacate the haze of my imagination and I'm back here, at the sandcastle. The breeze has grown colder and the water's icy bite is catching up with me, rain having already

32

soaked my face. My feet are numb and the wind is trying to push me back as I look at the waving, long grass of the dunes. I've been here before, throwing shells at the foam-crested waves. I've been here before.

I see that the little girl who played with the castle has returned and noticed the additional gravestones. She's brought a friend slightly smaller than her and they're moving the headstones around, and then using them to build another bridge over the moat. In awe, I watch their little fingers poke more windows into the structure and even more scrupulously, positioning a tiny twig on the top to represent a flagpole. They laugh, then leave, running towards the distant silhouette of a dog and its owner.

I crouch once again, to strike the wooden pencil against each glass before me. The final glimmer of sun is coruscating through the blistered pattern and as the rain drops into each small current, it permeates with a dull tap in different notes to create an odd scale. My glass harmonica has begun to play itself, bases beginning to agitate in the wet sand of the overflowing tide before the froth is soon the same height in every tumbler, the heads of white horses bobbing above the surface then galloping over the sides. Feeling water splash up to my palms, I stand up straight again.

My feet are now covered in water and with each new lap of the sea's tongue, it's rising up to my ankles, so I step backwards, away from the tide, only the eight, faint circles visible in a line in front of me.

'You want to get yourself dried off,' interrupts a voice and I at first think it's in my head. 'I've been waiting here for you all morning!' The gravel of this voice is familiar, crackly like that of a habitual cigar smoker. As I look at him, his stern smile disappears under the thick, white moss of his eyebrows, the leftover laverbread tarring his teeth.

'Bampa, what are you doing?' I link his arm and try to guide him away from the water.

33

'I walk here every day,' he says.

This was true about five years ago. I see how content his face is, something of an old independence creeping into the wrinkles. 'You want to get yourself dried off,' he repeats, peering down at my feet for longer than is necessary, from a face perched upon the wrappings of a large scarf.

'I walk here all the time,' he is saying again. 'I walk here all the time.' His face has turned sanguineous from excessive sea breath. He begins to look around and his feet start to get wet too, the leather of his shoes growing darker. 'Lovely,' he says and I wonder how much he means it. I can just about see the outline of Mumbles Lighthouse in the distance, the light here is fading quickly now.

One by one, I pick up each glass of water and tip it back into the tide. Sludges of sand that were stuck stubbornly inside are dropping out with a dense flop. I stack the glasses in my rucksack with no time to wrap them safely, the water already reaching my knees.

'I walk here all the—' my grandfather continues, but I interrupt him.

'Come on, Bamp,' I say. I link arms with him and we begin to walk along the bay, our trousers weighty from rain and seawater.

'Abertawe,' he sighs, idling sideways. He hunches ever so slightly but has a back so broad that it manages to centre the gravity of us both. The rain beats heavier but our pace remains the same as the tide continues to nag at our feet. I think of the evenings I've watched it roar with laughter, felt its saliva spitting onto my own, its lines creasing its corners into my memory, the wet tremble of the sea's palm broadening and nursing my malady to sleep.

Lady Venetia

It had been ten years since Martino's father was carried towards San Michele in a funeral boat; the buzz of the modern motor drowned out by the sound of the wind and water. At the time, it felt as though Venice really was the whole world, the living and the dead separated only by a lagoon.

Born into that steady sway, Martino had expected nothing less than to inherit his father's gondola, guiding tourists along the Canal Grande and singing barcarolles to the open air. Recently, however, he'd felt too reeled in by the seductive city, unsteadied by the familiarity of its acoustics and gothic architecture, and instead, every day, when the traffic lights turned red, he found himself staring at the grey waterlines on the walls of backstreet buildings that looked flaky to him now.

There, he would wait for the couples who were long-caught in photographs on the Ponte di Rialto, to flop into his floating crescent moon, and he'd avert his eyes every time they caressed upon the red, velvet love-seat. It hadn't taken long for the city to become a maze he knew every corner of, every calle, ruga and ramo, (which meant dead end), even every grey pigeon to have swindled salami from a terrified tourist as the ripe stench of sewage rose up from water too murky for reflections. Martino was sometimes requested to sing songs from Southern Italy, and with the Euros slapped into his hand, he had no choice but to sing 'O Sole Mio' over and over again.

He was still dressed in his black and white uniform when he stood at the water's edge, soaking up the Lido di Venezia, but instead of the single oar in his hand, he twirled a shell between his fingers and held it to his face as though absorbing every facet. It was the shape of a harp and yet he heard no sound anywhere near as beautiful as the music he'd once heard plucking the heartstrings of passers-by in Piazza San Marco. He hurled the shell as far as he could, not hearing how it dropped so tersely into the sea's breath but noticing how quickly it had escaped his palm. *This is real,* he thought, staring at the sea's rolling tongue, *this is the engine of it all*, and with slow, sunken breaths, he stepped forward, following his own strength.

The sea lingered around Martino's knees for a while, then his waist and his chest as he stood tall within it, until eventually, only his burnt-olive face could be seen above the water. While the waves took over, Martino closed his eyes and allowed his body to be lulled up and down.

Why won't he swim? the merwoman wondered, as she kept watch. She'd seen people do this before, seen them splash around like little dogs, then swim back in, but Martino's head was rolling with the waves, back and forth as the froth threw it around, his body, limp seaweed escaping beneath the surface, *unique seaweed, at least,* she thought, as she felt hundreds of fish smothering her flipper.

She could see far with those eyes, and sometimes disliked what she saw; the sea was a grey and dangerous place and her tail had been stabbed by hooks too many times over the years, which made it look more scaled than it should. That man, his eyes were closed and yet she was sure he wasn't dead because his arms were surrendered above him as though he hung upon one of the washing lines she sometimes saw trailing from window to window of the city-houses. Finding herself at this man's side, she could see that his mouth wasn't open but pursed closed as the waves washed over him and his boatish boots sank deeper and deeper. Embracing him was only just manageable around such a

36

large chest that she hoped was still beating as she hauled him to shore.

At a secluded part of the bay, her long and fleshy fishtail wrapped around Martino's body. The soothing breath of the sea kept him slumberous as he readjusted his furrowed head upon what he thought was a smooth and sinkable pillow, but after settling down to sleep again, it began to wriggle beneath him. Whenever he tossed and turned, the pillow tossed and turned too and there was a scent seeping into his dream, too hypnotic to ignore. He unpeeled his eyes to the balmy air and the muskiness grew more intense as he saw the teal scales beneath his cheek, the bare chest emerging from them before the beautiful face, which smiled as though it could bear any amount of sadness in the world.

Her peridot eyes held a curious daze that tilted her head to the side as they looked at him with the same, haunting beauty as a Venetian mask, and seeing the golden hair stir around her face, the scene seemed to blur more with each strand, causing Martino to fall forward into a kiss. *Was this vision living? Was it breathing?* With his eyes closed for another moment, Martino could smell that hypnotic scent even stronger than before; the merwoman's tongue warm and gritty with the salt from the sea. He saw that her arms had risen above her head, crossed over to resemble the antennae of a butterfly, her tail fluttering from the circular dip of sand their bodies had created. She could see every tired line in his face, the eyes of a young man sunken somewhere within, yet so real compared to her own, glistening beauty.

'So beautiful,' he whispered, resting the side of his face on the merwoman's stomach, unable to resist stroking the sea creature along the arc of her hip and then back up, slowly pressing her skin and then her scales, now shining diamantés of water. Hearing her insides gurgle back to him, he turned onto his knees and began to kiss lower regardless of her trembling, until she

37

unwound, her eyes closing and lips parting. As Martino reached the pointed ends of her fin, she giggled and rolled onto her stomach, her tail flapping around and flicking sand over his knees. There she was, the woman from another world, so serene. He was entirely allured by her and for the first time, he felt flooded with hope; if only she would be part of his future, he could forget the life he'd had alone.

Sprawled alongside each other, Martino stared at the precious tail that dipped into the tide; it would be perfectly statuesque for the city he knew. He'd heard plenty of myths and legends about mermaids, but this was different, she was so convincing, not human, of course, but definitely the highest form of woman he'd ever known. Thoughts drifting unknowingly into words, he imagined the merwoman lying next to him, not on the sandy shore but 'on land,' he mumbled. They could 'watch the ballet together,' listen to orchestras and 'make love to the' rising crescendo of passing gondolerie, while those diamantés of hers would sparkle, reminding him of his richness, 'of Venice's rich–'

'Stop it,' a little voice said abruptly, so high-pitched that it couldn't help but sound sweet. 'I'm flattered but I already—'

'You can speak?' asked Martino. The merwoman's eyelids dropped towards the sand and she began tracing shapes with her fingers; moons, lots of them, crescent moons, or were they gondolas? There she was, sparkling again; what would she ever need to be scared of?

Martino lifted the merwoman's chin with his fingers, relieved that she was still smiling, even if it wasn't the sure smile of before. She tilted her head to the side and rested her fingertips on his shoulders until he felt a warmth course through his body. What kind of gift would suit a woman who already had eyes as entrancing as Murano glass? Images of the both of them sailed through his mind: in a bathtub, in a swimming pool, even night swims in the bay seemed shallow when compared with the vastness of the sea she was used to, but he couldn't help but sink into thought.

The merwoman had sat up and her tail was curled to one side, the curve of her hip teasing him, and again seeing the impressions of each gondola drawn into the sand between them, Martino took one of her hands into his own.

'My houseboat,' he said, then brought her closer, 'you can stay there, with me!' This idea had initially lacked glamour, but they could stay there until they found a better solution. 'We can eat pizzas and pasta and drink wine until the late hours!'

'What about my—?' The little voice was asking a question and stroking where her knees would have been. She felt herself drying up, just thinking of it all.

'Your tail?' Martino asked. 'Well, you can dip it in and out of the water whenever you wish,' he added.

'I eat—'

Martino nodded. 'Anything you need, to stay as happy as you are right now,' and he stroked her fin as though it was the soft palm of a human hand. The merwoman beamed as the tide swept over her fin and his feet. She curled around Martino as tightly as an eel and the air grew cold with the shadow of the moon creeping over them.

When the sky was black, and the only lights were the clusters of lanterns outlining the lagoon, Martino heaved the merwoman along the beach and waved to a water taxi. The merwoman's arms draped over the back of Martino's shoulders; luckily, her tail almost-invisible as it followed Martino's feet. The pilot rolled his eyes with a cheeky smile as though it was all the result of an evening of too much wine, then steered them from Lido to Central Venice.

Martino's houseboat was sitting calmly upon the water of San Giorgio before he stumbled into it, his feet running as he flopped the merwoman down onto the bed in the bunker, its springs shrieking from the weight. Alone with him once again, she expelled a sigh, her arms lurching by her sides instead of embracing him. She began to draw breath, her chest frantically fluttering, but her face disclosing no pain.

'I'm sorry,' Martino whispered, 'but we're finally here.' Without speaking, the merwoman's arm reached out to the bedside table, her back struggling to sit up as her fingers pointed across the bedside— to the bottle. She needed water, of course. Martino handed it to her and watched her gilled neck pulsating as the liquid disappeared and the bottle slipped from her palm. Martino then filled a bowl with water and placed it on the floor beside her, so she could splash herself as she pleased. He lay down beside her and soon, they were both asleep.

When Martino awoke, the sun through the window was casting a fleece of heat across his body. Everything below his pelvis was barnacled to the merwoman's tail and the sensation led him to believe he was still mid-kiss upon the beach. Eventually opening his eyes, he recalled the entrancement of last night's journey and his body ached. The woman of his reverie was there alongside him, her eyes tightly closed. He kissed her lips, ready for the same, spirited woman she had been the day before but there was no movement.

Martino quickly stood up to splash her with water, but as his pelvis twisted to the side of the bed, it peeled away a layer of the merwoman's tail as easily as apple skin, exposing the raw scales underneath. Her body didn't flinch, the rest of her tail already crisped up like cooked mackerel upon the bed sheets. The merwoman emitted no teal sheen at all but only appeared as the kind of grey that would camouflage against a rocky bay.

His heart racing, Martino acquired a large bucket from the deck and began to fill it up. Then, trying to keep his balance as he returned, he set it down at the end of the merwoman's fin, which was dishevelled like a collage of slowly-detaching toenails.

Martino's hands shook as he frantically ladled the water along her body, the musky scent of her deterioration beginning to overwhelm him. Then he settled on his knees and, using a towel, wrung it out inches above her stomach so the drops landed upon her like heavy rain with the beads of sweat from his brow.

Nevertheless, the merwoman's figure was gradually shrinking, withering away within what had once looked like a small bed. Martino ladled more water over her, angry at the way in which it seemed to dissolve into nothing when it landed on her skin, then, disconsolate, he tipped the whole bucket over her body, hoping it would shock her into being. It made no difference, and so he perched on the edge of the space she'd left for him, his head in his hands as he began to moan aloud.

The tears fell from his eyes and without turning around, not bearing to look at the woman he'd so recently fallen in love with, he touched her with a tearful hand and was sure he felt some spirit in her tail. At first he'd assumed it was the twitching muscles of his tired arm, but glancing to his left, he saw the fin quivering, then beginning to wriggle and as he turned around, he heard a groan, the groan of someone awaking, stretching both her body and her voice. He then peered up at the merwoman, her arms were rising above her smiling face and her tail was stretching towards him.

'What a wonderful way to be awoken,' she sighed. Her precious sparkle had returned.

Sitting out on the deck, the air felt cooler. The merwoman draped her tail over the side to keep the end chilled by the water but wore a dress just long enough to disguise her scales; an old, green gown of Martino's mother's. On board, her body had no choice but to lie in a way that complimented itself, curled on its side, which would make anyone 'ordinary' look vulnerable, but the merwoman was anything but that; she had an air of power about her. Then she heard a sound close by. *Snap.* It was sharp and too quick to catch. A shark, perhaps? She hadn't come into contact with one for many years. Feeling afraid, she was about to ask Martino what it was but his hand was already spread across the bottom of her back and rotating her towards it.

Snap.

'Smile that beautiful smile of yours,' Martino whispered in her ear, displaying his teeth like a bracelet of pearls as she witnessed long threads of people appearing beside the canal, holding objects that flashed and flashed and flashed. 'Smile for the camera!' Martino repeated, louder this time. 'Lady Venetia,' he exclaimed, stepping a few feet away from her and opening his right arm to present her sitting there. As she embraced the smiles and returned her own, she examined the deck at the front of the boat and saw there were letters painted: two words, it seemed, with a gap between them. *Lady Venetia,* she repeated quietly to herself.

Snap went the flash of another camera, and then another as the summer-clad tourists gathered as though Lady Venetia was someone unworldly. They became smaller, almost miniscule as Martino continued steering them along the canal but remained close to the side for all to see her. She was startled by another crowd of tourists waving, trying to attract her attention from a nearby bridge and other people from an approaching boat. *Snap*, then another flash and Martino waved back but as he took his second hand away from the wheel, the boat began to edge to the left and too close to the wall of the Giudecca Canal.

Forgetting this wasn't a gondola, Martino scrambled to the side of the boat and placed his hand on the wall as if it would be enough to stop them drifting inwards. He realised his mistake too late because his arm twisted into a sharp angle, and as Venetia and the tourists watched in terror, there was a giant *snap*, then a shriek when Martino finally lost his balance. When he fell into the water, the boat scraped and knocked against the canal wall, jamming him in between, the sound of his one-handed splashes and gasps for air fading, and his face becoming hardly visible above the surface. Then a large waterbus passed by, causing the waves to pound against the already-rocking houseboat. Lady Venetia clambered to the side of the deck where he struggled, her dress tearing open and exposing her scaly tail to the screaming jaw of every tourist.

The merwoman searched for Martino and found the top of his head, which she used to haul his whole body upwards. As the boat continued to move forward, she flopped sideways into the water, clinging onto him with all the strength she had, leading them away as Martino's flattened and disfigured body wept blood into the canal. In each other's arms for a second time, she used the power of her tail to wash them up onto the side. Wrapping her scales softly around him, she knew those eyes would never stare at her again and so she closed hers too, never wanting to wake up. Venice continued to move around them and the tourists continued to gather.

When Lady Venetia did wake up, she felt no sun at all. Instead, there was a very different light beaming down upon her body; a blindingly white light that made her feel weak and dehydrated. Opening her eyes a little, she saw that her wrists were strapped down either side of her. She tried to free them but the leather only pinched her skin.

'Don't try that, dear. It'll help you more if you remain calm.' Lady Venetia shook her head as though the voice was caught inside. Then she felt its breath on her face, warm like the light upon her skin and just as discomforting. It smelled foggy, too, like risen stomach acid allowed to stagnate. Lady Venetia shut her eyes again as though it would erase the odour, but as she did, the footsteps walked around her.

It had been a woman's voice, she felt sure, but the footsteps sounded more like a man's. Lady Venetia opened her eyes again and could just about see a face so perfect that there was

43

something uneasy about it: the unblemished olive skin, the accurately kinked and parted chestnut hair and eyes, nose and lips, so symmetrical. The top of the face was outlined with sharply-angled eyebrows and her face didn't move as the voice escaped it.

'You're in Ospedale, the research quarter.'

The woman took a pen from the pocket of her white coat and began to make markings over the merwoman's body. She began to panic when she felt the coldness of the wet nib drawing lines across her face and from her navel to her fin. It was easier to keep her eyes closed when the light only pained her. More people entered the room; she could hear their voices.

'Hybrid human being' they called her and they began to talk of terrifying things, such as reconstructing her tail into two human legs, using her peeled-off scales to cover merchandise, or alternatively, to undertake a prompt taxidermy. *What was that?* She couldn't bear to listen anymore, so she thought about Martino, how he had kissed every inch of skin where the ink lay.

She thought more about his crumpled body, the way she'd wrapped his dead arms around her to try and recreate what they had been together. She'd begun to miss him as soon as she'd seen the boat pummelling his broad body and rugged face, leaving an empty vessel with no love, no breath and no kisses to give her. How strange that he'd existed enough to be held by her, yet not long enough to belong to her. Upon that reflection, an unusual tingling began in her face, a little like a tiny jellyfish stinging her skin. Puddles appeared in her eyes and with her hands tied, she couldn't wipe them away, so she began to whimper.

'What have we here?' the woman asked, her mocking head levitating above the merwoman's. 'Marco, look. The mutant appears to be crying.' Her voice spoke more loudly and echoed through the hospital room before her mouth squirmed into a sideward smile. Her eyes didn't stop staring into Lady Venetia's tears as they flowed, and she allowed one to drop onto her palm like a delicate jewel.

Following this, Marco touched the cheek of Lady Venetia more brashly, her frightened face convulsing at his fingertips. Then her eyes poured out tears so fast that they no longer had time to crawl down her cheeks. Instead, they spurted out like pearly projectiles.

The surgeons ordered the merwoman to remain calm but she was out of control: the more they examined her, the more she began to cry; her grief for Martino was catching up with her. She was sure she could hear a slight shake in the voice of the woman in white; something odd was happening to Lady Venetia's hands: they prickled as they did in the sea when her fingers crinkled, then they began to feel softer, with a jelly-like sensation. As her back arched itself, water began to spray from her fingertips now stretched like turgid starfish in front of her.

She heard the surgeons' voices beginning to scream, heard their feet starting to wade through what sounded like gallons, then torrents of water as her bed dislodged from the ground and instead began to float. She cried more, as it began to spin around and around, the light less intense upon her skin as the room grew dark, then light, then dark, then light and the dizziness hit her as she heard the voices spinning in the distance, treading water and gasping for air.

Then, other than the sound of gushing tears, there was silence. With the force of the water, Lady Venetia's bed broke from the room and pushed itself through the swing doors, down the corridors and out of the hospital wing. She let out a wail so loud that it echoed throughout the building, the tears rising around the walls. She couldn't feel her body by now, it felt so at one with the water, which was trying to seep out of her arms, her torso and her tail. Even though she was still strapped down, this felt slightly akin to swimming.

The hospital doors spat the merwoman out of the building and onto the surface of her heightened sadness, along with everything else it could carry, which included people who couldn't survive the force. As the tears rose, so did she, the canals losing all definition, not a bridge to be seen, and the city of Venice becoming unrecognisable beneath her and the blue mirror of the sky. The sun was warm upon her saturated face, too warm for her really, but it soothed her cries, which ceased to tremble through her body until her skin became parched upon the hospital bed. The water had risen so high that the dead were already floating, accompanied by rats who swam alongside.

In the absence of Venice's sirens, Lady Venetia began to sing. Cold and lonely notes poured from her mouth, elongated and high-pitched like some apocalyptic lullaby. At first, it was two, soothing notes, *duuuuhhhhhh, DUHHHHHHHH, duuuuhhhhhh, DUHHHHHHH,* tinny like a large wind chime at the top of a bell tower. Then there were three notes, then four, eventually slowing down to the low tone of a toll bell as though to drain the city of any love.

As the water started to level off, it carried her past the dead island of San Michele, much of its stony face still beneath the blue, the water seeping through the graveyard. Soon, she realised her bed had carried her to the bay where she had met Martino. She thought of them stretched alongside one another; that affectionate look in his eyes. Then the waves seemed to grasp her more firmly as she drifted backwards, thrown higher than before, the bed frame breaking away and setting her free to be caught in the water's hands.

Finally, she sprung into the air, curved into a rainbow and leapt head first into the blue, her hair a blonde train behind her as she returned to the depths. The floating city had sunk once again, been anaesthetised by a single woman, so the ashen faces of tourists were piled up wherever the water decided as it slowly began to sink. Unlike the scattered fish, the merwoman continued to swim, her tail quivering behind her as she dived deeper. Rising up, the sun on Lady Venetia's face felt pleasant now, as her tail trod water, keeping her balanced above the surface just enough to look back at all she had done: forever floating, forever sinking.

Black and Yellow

I stole a sieve from the kitchen because it was the closest to a microscope I could find, then tucked it beneath the back of my braces where they crossed against my shirt. I can smell the sieve now, old flour must have glued itself to the metal. I wanted to see the way some insects see, you know, with multiple lenses. The mosaic of light would filter through the dulled, silver weave and if I closed one eye, then I would be able to see fragments of the real thing through each, tiny square.

I was running so fast with it around my face that I forgot to keep track of where my feet were going, almost crashing into my father's Ford Anglia parked behind the big barn. It was thanks to the field full of bright dandelions catching my eye that I eventually allowed my monocle to drop to the ground. I couldn't ignore the colour. It was only then that I saw what I'd been looking for; polka dots of red and black scuttling across the grass. I slowly lifted my heel and then my toe to check if anymore were hiding. No harm done, I thought, no harm done. Then I lifted my other foot and at the sight of yellow blood, felt the veins pumping in my wrist. I hadn't only stepped on one, I'd spliced it in half like a broken domino.

The ladybird was distorted in such a way that I'd placed its head upon the moving body of another. I remember wondering if the heads of insects could be transplanted. Maybe that would happen, I thought, which made me feel less guilty for a moment. The ladybird twitched and continued its journey up the bark of the tree, carrying the black speck of the dead bug's head along with it. In its defence, it was beginning to send out a bitter smell, like unripe tomatoes.

After that, even though my feet felt firmly rooted where they were, I knew I had to do something, so I peeled a leaf from the tree that hung over me and covered the remaining body as neatly as I could. I remember imagining a butterfly exploring the farm with a ladybird's head and I felt optimistic for a while.

Only metres away, mum was pacing up and down row upon row of vegetables. Every day, they looked larger and greener. I'd been watching more closely lately and noticed that the taller they grew, the more arguments they caused: my parents blamed each other for dry spells and 'unwanted visitors'.

My brother was less interested, usually more consumed by the buzzing of his radio, which I often heard talking from his room late at night. He was more taken with mechanical things, he liked to drive around on our Massey Ferguson or just tip me out of a wheelbarrow every now and then. I tried to stick around, find out what all the fuss was about. I found it fascinating how some crops perished while the others grew up to be what we'd be eating on our plates a few weeks later.

I walked over to mum as though nothing had happened. Dad had shown me how to join in with the planting, so I thought I'd be able to help. He sometimes gave me my own shovel to dig into the soil and I'd grunt the same way he did as I sunk my foot onto the metal square, bringing up old roots. Sometimes, I'd see creatures crawling from beneath the earth, a worm slowly stretching out, then allowing the rest of its body to catch up with itself, and a song from Sunday School would come to mind: 'All things bright and beautiful, all creatures great and small.'

When I arrived at mum's side, it was clear that it was a day to check up on everything, which was much easier. I stood there for a while, watching her lift the leaves of recently-grown fruit plants in the same manner that she used to wave her hand between silky skirts in dress shops at the weekend. She seemed relaxed until I heard her voice; it was so loud all of a sudden.

'Well, well.' Then there was a gasp, so I knew we were in trouble. It meant either that the leaves were brown, nothing had grown at all or even worse, that something had been eaten.

My grumbling stomach automatically made me consider my brother's greedy eating habits, but it turned out that mum wasn't actually accusing any of us. Instead, she was holding the palm of her hand wide open in front of my face and tipping it left and right as she sometimes did with a frying pan.

As I tilted my head towards her tilting hand, I saw something moving in the very centre of her lifeline; it was black and yellow, as bright as the dandelions and curled up in such a way that it looked like the body of a bee. At first, I panicked, thinking there had been another tragedy, but then it moved, and I didn't need a microscope because as it unravelled, I could see that it did have feet, they were tiny specks of black along the bottom and its hairy, stretched-out body was just over the length of my little finger. It began to slither across my mother's palm, head dipping down into another lifeline, then rising up and carrying the rest of its body with it, as swimmers do in water.

She kept tipping her hand to keep hold of it, but it was becoming more awkward, moving a little faster, most likely quite scared.

'You've been eating our food, haven't you, dear?' she was whispering to it as she began to walk away, but as she was about to place the creature elsewhere, I ran after her. My face was burning again; I just couldn't let her, not this time. As the black and yellow reached the edge of her hand, I opened both of mine alongside for extra land for it to explore. After it crossed over, mum smiled and went back to checking the other crops. I realised that with two hands, I could nicely manoeuvre wherever this creature decided to go.

Our home wasn't enormous; the amount of land was about twenty acres, maybe twenty-two but it was enough to lose yourself in. Leaving mum to her examination of the crops, I began to carefully walk away from the field and toward the next, keeping a watch on the black and yellow tickling the skin of my palms. Now I had it, I didn't know what to do with it, so I kept walking, sure that I'd eventually find a place where it would be allowed to reside.

I began to feel hungry myself, so I made my way back to the house, ignoring the chickens that clucked at me as I reached the back door. I cut through the scullery, then carefully, without looking up from my hands, walked upstairs and placed the caterpillar in a small mug I'd left on my bedroom windowsill. Dinner wouldn't be long; I could already smell the wholesome, rich potatoes cooking and I hoped it was mash, I always had an appetite for mash.

At the kitchen table, the four of us sat and without sharing any words other than, 'Will you pass the potato please?' we ate everything. I always forgot until I ate mash, how much I understood my brother's lust for food. I saw his face, rosy with the lack of oxygen he was taking in as he engulfed each, soggy spoonful, the gravy dribbling down his chin like a second tongue, and as he noticed it, the lug of his bare, chubby wrist wiping it away.

I ate more slowly than he did, something I could tell from the noise of his jaw opposite me. I liked to savour it a little more, the mush of mash that felt like baby food on my taste buds. There was no technique involved with a food so lazy, so willing to cling to the roof of my mouth. On the plate, it lost its height like a molehill does. All our cutlery clinked together within seconds of each other, mine last. I remember, there were no arguments.

Since food hadn't taken too long, I knew there would be plenty of time to check on my friend before bedtime, so I went to the bathroom sink, quickly washed my face before the water had a chance to turn warm and put my striped pyjamas on. Then I ran up to my room, turned the light on and shut the door behind me.

I closed the window, and then carefully picked up the mug from the sill with both hands. Instead of bringing it towards me, I shimmied my feet forward and leaned my head over it. There staring back at me was an empty, brown base with only the ring of unlicked milk around the rim. I blinked again and opened my eyes wider in case I was missing the obvious wriggle of black and yellow, but there were no stripes to be seen.

After setting the mug down on the windowsill once again, I sat myself on the end of the bed and cried, thinking of the red and black and the black and yellow, and wishing they could exist together somewhere. Maybe they would. Mum clicked the door open and not noticing the tears on my cheeks, said, 'Aw, you're all ready for bed! Well done, boy.' I didn't smile back. She walked towards the window, picked up the mug and kissed me on the forehead. 'I'll take this downstairs where it's supposed to be.' That was when I felt my eyes filling up again, but her back had already turned. 'Night love,' she said, as the door clicked shut. I mumbled back, 'Night,' then heard her feet slowly descend the stairs.

Knowing I could have asked her to help me look for my friend, made my stomach hurt, but she wouldn't have understood my getting so upset over a caterpillar. I remember sitting on the edge of my bed, scanning the rug and the pattern of the lino for black and yellow, but there were so many tears that, after a few minutes of trying, I gave up and turned off the light.

I sat upon the giant flower sewn into the bedspread and sobbed until it was light outside, then crawled into the cold wrappings of the bed sheets, crossed my arms around each other, trying not to shiver too much, and buried my face in my chest. It wasn't long before I felt my body slowly heating up as the sunlight poured in; the quilt forming a cocoon around me.

Searching for the Fog

The window is slammed shut before I can move my nose out of the way; the fog's tears mid-shiver upon my skin. Here we are again, the fog and I, only separated by pane. *Don t go outside* says the window. *Come outside* says the fog, as a pair of silver palm prints grow visible on the glass, gradually shrinking to display a pair much smaller, the digits disappearing, one by one.

'He's not here, Claire,' says my mother.

'And he's not going to—' my sister doesn't say the rest before peeling me away.

They're a smog all of their own, but they're right, he definitely isn't coming back.

It takes hours, but eventually, their voices fade. I have to balance on the edge of the porch, struggling to lift my arm to a convincing farewell and hope they're too far up the street to scrutinise my sorry attempt at a smile. When they leave, I'm thankful it's just us again; the door left wide open to my other obligation.

This, I know, is the perfect time to search for the fog. There's something about the rain. The prickle of its droplets softens so quickly upon my face that they're almost indistinct. They seep into my skin like soggy parasites and I'm happy to submit as they soak up every second thought from my head. Then, with their hospitable weight, they draw me further outside and towards my hibernating car, where I find myself scraping ice from the windscreen. Beginning up the street, the engine takes a while to revive itself from its unconscious state, and then finally returns

55

to belting out tunes as though it had never been on stop for so many months: one singer joining me all the way from the eighties, the melody bouncing, lamb-like after her voice. On my approach to the mountain, the sheep at the roadside aren't quite so delicate, their eyes pairs of yellow zircon, glaring at me. I turn up the volume, so the singer becomes my bellowing passenger, hired to make this appropriately dramatic.

Now it's just me and sound on the road, driving my dream through the Betws Mountain. My seatbelt isn't buckled but hanging limply by my side. Why would I need it? No, I relax my shoulders and rest my fingers on the steering wheel, no grip is necessary. Ah, there's the darkness infringing as I start down this familiar country lane, curling past a pale cottage where a guard goose waddles after the car, only amusing me with its warning. The tall hedges either side are narrowing the lane; I drag my car to the left-hand side, and then drag it back, feeling the first thrill.

The feathery hedges really hide the prize: it's just one curved corner after another, one blind spot after another, but I can see something else in the distance: the fog. There it is again, its fingertips are reaching out to me with silvery nails that wither away as I drive towards them. I know this is the right direction, I can see its body, its embrace drawing me in with all-consuming arms. I'm not at the fog yet but it's already smothering everything so seductively in that smoky, cosy blanket. How does it do that? It invites me in with the same charm as the pillow I used to sink my head into. *He's not here, Claire,* say that family of mine, probably still saying it now, low and clearly as my lips mouth the same words to the mist-filling windscreen. I drive on through the transparency.

The road ahead of me is becoming invisible and the sharp turn has already approached. A second away from becoming part of the blur, I imagine my car being hauled over the top of the Betws and into the haze. A tear is created in each eye: I can't believe this is finally taking place. However, no accident happens, no tragedy at all. Instead, my hands turn the wheel to the right, so I swing the car around the corner and begin to descend a slope. It doesn't feel half as dangerous as it should. I'm so close to the edge but there's a grey screen hiding the view of the Amman Valley and its dotted houses, so it feels more enclosed like an outdoor corridor or a fence keeping me in. I'm calm, controlled even as I continue to coast into the widening throat of the Betws. I can't stop peering over the side, attempting to see through the grey. *He's not here, Claire,* they'd kept telling me. I know he's not here, that's the problem, I'm not quite there yet.

As I glance into the rear-view mirror, I see the car filling with silent, disapproving relatives. I adjust it and they blur, but I also see something emerging out of the vaporous road in front of me; a pair of headlights without a car. They're glazed with a drunken cloudiness, yet pursuing me like curious cats' eyes that have strayed from their street. *He's not here, Claire,* recites over and over in my head. I wish they'd shut up. I wish they'd smothered me with a pillow through the night so I'd stop hearing those same, burdensome words; I feel like the fog, undistinguishable underneath. I glance at the rear-view mirror once again and realise the eyes have disappeared and a bottle-green bonnet is hovering into view. I slow down to thirty miles per hour as my heart ticks more quickly.

I can hear myself breathing heavily through my nose, and my teeth are aching from being clenched together, not from fear but rapid excitement. The rocking back and forth of the car behind makes me linger for longer on the narrow road, turning up the radio and winding down my window to let the air in. As the car slowly overtakes, I take the brief opportunity to ask its driver the one, inevitable question.

'What's the quickest way to the fog?' I shout with a palm at the side of my mouth. His weather-roasted face scrunches up into a look of pressed perplexity, then he begins to speed up. There's no time to observe, he's already gone and I can see the fog looming in the distance like the dust that unfurls from a quarry. The nose of his car is disappearing into it, just the predator's tail lights tiring and closing before becoming nothing. I can feel my face burning with frustration again. *He's not here, Claire,* I whisper to myself before driving on, the speedometer fluttering up to fifty.

After a while, I can see the viewing point especially for the fog. The bottle-green vehicle is parked there alone, so I stop right next to it, my car puffing out a sigh. There's a picnic bench ahead of me, miserably slanted to one side. Here, I unlock the doors so the metal barrier diminishes between our two vehicles but even though I'm alone, I don't feel nervous at all. When I step out of the car, the air is humid and the wind is moist, just like the breath of someone close upon my cheek.

I walk towards the edge. I can hear footsteps behind me, so I turn around to see the man with the roasted face clutching a bouquet of flowers to his chest; they look like lilies. He's carrying them as though they're freshly picked for the occasion and I don't care that he's offering me one with his outstretched arm. His head is raised as though preparing for a profound speech to fall from his mouth. I take the flower without a thank you and hold it between two hands. It feels so fragile, its scent is sweet and green, yet musty like the fog as it grazes upon the grassy hills, comforting but bringing sadness to me that I want more of. I remember that smell seeping up my nostrils when I was somewhere else, holding on tightly to those little hands. The man is watching me now, as I close my eyes, then open them again.

'We used to sit here to watch the sunset when we first met,' he's saying, breaking my thoughts with his own and placing the rest of his flowers on the miserable bench next to us. 'Can I ask what's wrong?' He seems calm but the tongue-to-teeth sound of his speech makes him sound irate. Examining the texture of his face, I say nothing, my arms left to lilt at my side. 'Whatever it is, you can tell me, you know. I've been through all sorts,' he adds, his eyes trying to burn into mine. I look away as I feel them beginning to water, but I still say nothing.

The silence seems unbearable to him; he's widening his stance into that of an upside-down 'Y'. This conversation or lack thereof reminds me of being a lacklustre teenager but it can't be helped, the words are just dissolving in my head.

'Don't tell me, you're feeling sorry for yourself,' he says, staring. 'People like you make me sick.' Now, he's turning around, muttering messed-up words to himself and kicking the mud ahead of him with his big, heavy boots, his hands clawing onto his pockets. 'Then there are people like me. I'd do anything to see my wife again,' he shouts, standing metres away. I suddenly feel small and useless again, here at the edge of the fog. I look at the woeful bench and feel my body bending the same way.

I'm fixated on his boots as they walk towards his car, flattening the grass as though I'm buried underneath.

'No,' I say, when it's too late and I speak with my chin down, too weakly for him to hear. I've not mentioned my little boy. As I glance up again, the man's car door slams, causing the scent of the flower to waft back and forth. I know what it feels like to want to do anything to heal the pain, to try and unstitch a memory until the thread is like coloured dust in your hands but you fall to pieces looking at it. That's what I want to say, but the green car has already disappeared. I place the flower alongside its bouquet.

Now he's gone, I have more time to think. I traipse back to my car, stand by its side and examine its blue body, still warm. I walk around to its boot and take out my raincoat, which feels chilled and hardened. Then I walk to investigate the map that stands proudly near the edge. Plainly, it says, 'You are here,' but there's no mention of the fog at all, which strikes me as bizarre considering the circumstances. I can see it ahead of me now.

There's something so comforting about it. It stands like a perfectly painted wall that you'd expect to walk up to and touch with your fingertips. You'd think you could rest the palm of your hand on its moist, ash grey paint, just as you could with a watercolour wash, the runny, coloured sky dropping onto your skin because it hasn't yet dried. I place a hand on either side of the map's wooden frame as I would with a lectern and I stare at the fog for a while. I want to drift into the past, to the way things used to be. I'm sure my boy is in that direction, I can feel it.

Whilst standing here, where I'd usually see the Amman Valley stretching for miles and miles beneath me, it's now disappeared under the fog, with only the distant halos of light struggling to peep through. Here, with the fog spitting second-hand rain at my face, I understand something for the first time: why people ever presumed the world was flat. Ahead of me is a wall dense enough to contain a door. I walk towards it, stopping between steps to appreciate its unshaken and overpowering presence. Then I press on, but my walk seems endless. Every inch of my surroundings is painted ash as though I'm trapped in a small but simultaneously vast room and can't possibly find my way back. I look straight ahead, not needing to close my eyes because there's nothing to see anymore. I only need to step out onto a great, big comforting cloud.

He's not here, Claire. He's not here, my mother and sister are saying again, but this time, I know they're wrong. I don't have to jump from the edge because there's no edge to be seen, so I just keep walking, my feet squelching through the grass beneath me. Eventually, my steps become silent. I consider that perhaps I've already fallen, and yet I haven't felt the rush of air above me. I'm waiting for those soft and clammy hands to take hold, but where are they? There's so much nothing. Where's my boy?

60

Tangerines

I heard that oranges have the power to make people happy. I've been eating tons of tangerines but when the fleshy fruit sits between my teeth, it reminds me of goldfish and I suddenly feel vegetarian. I also heard that goldfish aren't always dead when you find them floating on the top of water but sometimes only comatose.

I visit Nan with tangerines. She only lives a few roads away from us, so I walk there on my way home from school, then meet Mum inside, who's always whispering everything she says, as she flits around and smiles even though the house smells ill. Illness smells like rubber, or bad breath when you have a cold. Once, when Nan wasn't looking, I saw Mum spray some air freshener, but the breath still lingered everywhere. Mum says it can't be helped, especially since Nan's bed moved downstairs to the front room. It's easier for her without the climbing, plus, everything she needs is down here.

'Already on my way out,' Nan said when she was first moved, and her head kept laughing above the duvet. I didn't understand what was funny because she never really goes anywhere.

I know Nan really likes tangerines, or I thought she did because she always said grapes were too bland, but lately she looks disappointed with whatever she eats. A few weeks ago, she snatched one of the tangerines from me and rolled it around in her hand. For a while, we both watched it spin upon her palm, the bumpy face of it turning like I'd seen hers doing when she slept, then we watched it drop and roll across the carpet until it

61

nudged the little bone on my ankle and she gave me a gummy grin. We'd known it wouldn't bounce, but I think we'd both expected more of a thud.

Since Mum said 'help yourself to those tangerines', I've taken lots of them from the red bag on the kitchen table at Nan's house. When I first saw it, I asked what it was made from and Mum said she wasn't sure. I assumed it was crocheted because a lot of things at Nan's are crocheted. The kind of bag it is, reminds me of a net I saw on television; people were using it to catch fish from the sea, to scoop out hundreds of giant tuna. Then they sold them all to be eaten. It feels good when you scissor through the net to take a tangerine out because it's such a struggle otherwise; it's impossible to only use your hands, but once you've broken through, you can rip the rest as much as you like and the netting creaks as though you're breaking into something you're not supposed to.

When Nan paid more attention, I'd sit alongside her and peel the tough skin. Then I'd remove the white core; juice sometimes spits into your eyes when you do that. It bursts from the orange veins as you rip the white strings away. Then I'd peel each segment away, one by one, placing them upon Nan's palm and the next half-moon upon my own tongue. The bite felt like I was killing something but I wanted her to eat them.

Nan always talks about dying. Mum says she's very direct. *On my last legs* is one of her sayings, which always makes me picture her with more legs; an elderly centipede with a walking stick. *Over the hill* is another one, which sounds like an adventure, while *six feet under* definitely doesn't. Sometimes, she just says, *I'll be gone soon* and I wonder where she's going again because she doesn't look particularly happy about it. Then she reminds us of her age. Lately, she's *gone eighty*, so that must mean she's eighty-one. Her back springs up whenever Mum calls her a creaking door, *going on forever, but groaning about it*, as Dad says. Lately, Nan isn't groaning very much at all.

62

It's been months since I first brought Nan tangerines. This week, everyone's stopped me from going inside the front room, so I sit on the stairs instead. I can't wait until I'm allowed to see Nan. I've been peeling as many tangerines as I can, then leaving them outside the door of the front room. She used to peel them herself but she's always found it difficult, her thumbs are so curved with arthritis that she can't quite dig her nails into the skin.

The worst thing is when I find tangerines outside the door the next day and I can tell they haven't moved an inch, which has been happening a lot more, lately. I haven't stopped leaving them just in case Nan ever changes her mind. I've been peeling them as best as I can, splitting open the skin and leaving the wet segments in a little bowl of hers that's light enough to pick up. I wish I could see her enjoying them, sucking the orange juice from each mushy lump but I'm afraid that if I watch, it won't happen. Luckily, the last few days, the bowl's been empty again, so she must be glad that I still visit.

The night before last, I dreamt that I stared through a spyhole in the door while Nan was sleeping, but yesterday when I checked, it was the same, solid, oaky thing and I really missed her on the other side. Today, I checked again, traced my hand over the wood, but it was smooth with no sign of a hole beneath my fingers. There's no way I could have seen her, unless I was peeping from under the armpits of family; they keep pushing themselves through the gap whenever the door opens. Since growing up last month and being just like Mum, I thought I'd be allowed in, but they say, 'Let her rest, love, leave her sleep,' all smiles. Then they hand me the empty bowl as though I'm not a young woman at all, but just a child in the way.

'I *was* letting her rest,' I say, but they don't understand. Yesterday, only a slither of skin was left at the bottom of the bowl. Every time it's empty, I fill it up again. I'm trying to do as much for Nan as I can and it seems to be working at least a little bit. 'I am a young woman,' I say, but it makes no difference.

It's not fair that they're allowed to speak to Nan, allowed to watch her enjoying the fruit that *I* leave for her. I used to be able to hear her say, *bye love*, when they squeezed back through the gap, and I used to shout back, *bye Nan,* so she'd know I was always there but lately, everyone's either whispering or pressing fingers to their lips when they see me and I ask if Nan's okay.

'She's sleeping,' they say, 'she's sleeping.' Sometimes, I sit on the bottom stair and curl up with my head resting two steps above. I try to dream just as Nan must be, but the smell creeps into my sleep and I cling onto it until I open my eyes again and feel the pattern of the carpet printed onto my forehead.

Lately, I can't seem to eat any more tangerines. I used to finish them off myself when we shared them. I'd sit there, staring at the line of Russian Dolls on the windowsill when Nan hadn't said anything for a while, and I used to suck the orange blood from each one. It must be since I've been bleeding, it's put me off; the pips make me think of ovaries, everything makes me think of them. I watched a film at school that told us how three generations of women can contain the same egg and it made my stomach feel sick. I think of myself as an egg, lodged halfway down my mother's fallopian tubes like the blocked pipes in the bathroom, and then I imagine those pipes being forced inside my Nan's stomach in the same way they stuff the turkey at Christmas, so we're all squashed together at once.

This evening, they've left the front door of Nan's house open for more visitors, but before I can say cat, the street cat turns up beside me dressed in black with a white shirt for a chest. It's skulking around the hallway at the bottom of the stairs and stopping outside the door of the front room. Everything is so quiet here that the patter of paws is loud on the tiles. I think it might be sniffing for the same spyhole that I was looking for, so

I stand beside it, checking again. I press my face up against the wood but I still can't see anything. I hear crying though, it's coming from inside. They're wailing like the dog across the road sometimes does and it's made the cat jump back in the same way as it does when it sees the dog. It's coming from more than one person, but I can tell that one of those people is Mum. I feel angry because I don't want them to disturb Nan from her sleep, so I knock on the door.

'Hello? Is Nan okay?'

I only hear silence.

Somebody steps out and shoos the cat away; the lady seems as angry as I am.

'Oh! That cat's been eating the tangerines for days,' she says, and as I look at the cat again, tiptoeing over the threshold, I see that it's carrying a trail of tangerine skin in its mouth; a long, orange tongue is hanging from its jaw, dropping into tiny fragments. Thinking that I can't feel angrier and not knowing what else to do, I feel my eyes burning like they do when the tangerine juice sometimes sprays into them. I've taken so much time to peel it for Nan and it was the last one. This woman is giving me a hug and saying it will be okay but at the same time, she's still shooing the cat away.

'I'm your Great Aunty Amber, remember me?' I nod, but I really don't. The cat's looking back, stopping in its path.

'*Skkkkkt,*' she shouts after it again and then it scarpers.

'There's a new bag in the kitchen,' I say, 'I know there is, but they're too tough for even me to peel at the moment and Nan won't be able to chew or swallow them without her teeth. She might choke.' I try not to choke on my words, knowing how ridiculous it is to be upset about it all. I'm ten and a half now, a young woman.

Great Aunty Amber doesn't seem to respond this time but there's a sad look on her face, as if she's finally understood.

'Why hasn't Nan been eating the tangerines?' I ask, but she's squeezing a flower of tissues into her handbag. I run after the shadow of the cat and finding it curled upon the bonnet of a car that's recently parked up, I tear the tangerine skin away from its teeth before it throws a claw out to scratch me. I take it in my hand along with the remaining pieces, throw them in a bowl and follow my Great Aunty Amber into the kitchen where she says she'll sit with me for a while, until everyone else returns. The feet of the chairs scrape loudly against the tiles. Why hasn't Nan been eating the tangerines?

After a while of sitting with Great Aunty Amber and smiling back at her, I tell her that I'm going to the bathroom. While she puts the kettle on, I quickly cut open the new bag of tangerines and hide it under my jumper, then tiptoe away. I can't help but peel the skin from one of them. It takes a while but I remove its whole face, turning it in my hand as my other thumb draws a snake around the outside. I split what is left of the undressed tangerine in half, then tug the white strands away from its middle.

Seeing the white strings bunched together on my palm, reminds me of Nan and her sister's washing lines, all holding hands across the three gardens of their terraced houses, which makes me think of the three generations of women containing the same egg. Then I think about the Russian dolls on Nan's sill, how would the little one be able to survive without the bigger one, and how would the bigger one be able to survive without the largest one? My eyes start gushing again.

I stuff a tangerine into my mouth, whole. I plunge my teeth into it and feel the orange blood bursting out, some of the skin is in pieces but the rest of it turns soggy and takes a while to be chewed up. Once it's gone, I take another from the bag, pushing it into my mouth with my finger and thumb and then all of my knuckles. I'm in the habit of chewing now and without finishing it, I take another and try to cram it into the front of my mouth but there isn't enough space. I'm not even chewing anything anymore, I'm only swallowing the soggy tangerine in large lumps while tossing the peel into the toilet in front of me. I wonder if just like the goldfish, it will be swimming out at sea, or will it just float above the surface for while? At first, it seems to clog and go nowhere, groaning every time as I nag the chain, but after giving it a few minutes, I can see the water spitting back up and it burps into the echoing bathroom.

I can still hear the tremble of the water in the cistern. My stomach begins to tremble, too. I feel the most sick I have for a while; the living room door seemed to be shut more carefully after Great Aunty Amber had walked out of it and I could tell it wouldn't let anyone else in, not even me, even though I'm older now. Why did Nan stop eating the tangerines? I try stuffing another one into my mouth but there's just no room, and as I do, I feel a clutch of pips at the back of my throat, they're playing with my tonsils. My eyes are still wet and soon, I'm heaving like the cat dressed in black when it coughs up a hairball, then I'm retching. Eventually, a stream escapes my mouth and at the same time, I notice orange vomit, little fingernails of peel decorating the ceramic. I hear a knock at the door behind me.

I say nothing because I suddenly feel irritated by my Great Aunty Amber, who isn't great at all. They said that since I've become a young woman, I'm allowed to be irritated, but I'm worried I didn't lock the door properly, and I'm worried she'll barge in. I want to tell her to wait just a second, I want to say, 'Mum says I'm allowed my womanly privacy,' but the next heave happens without my control, the vomit thinner and the acidy taste burning the inside of my mouth. It makes me want to be sick and sick and sick but my throat is so tired that I can no longer even try to hold any of it back. I let it take my body with it, tugging at my stomach and emptying me into the basin.

Just as I'd dreaded, I hear the door behind me creaking open;

she's managed to twist open the flimsy lock. Retching again, I feel a hand on the back of my neck and then two hands holding back my hair and stroking it from the top of my head. At first, I try to shake them off because the hands are icy but at the same time, I don't dislike them.

'I know it's upsetting, love, but Nan's gone, now,' the voice is saying, but it doesn't belong to Great Aunty Amber at all, it's Mum. She doesn't sound as happy as before, but she does sound calmer. 'She's gone,' she says again, 'if you'd like to see her now, you can.' At this, I listen to my panting breath; it's slowed down but now it's speeding up again as my head hangs over what has left my body.

'Nan's gone,' she says again, and I feel how much blood has rushed towards my face. Gone where?

'Would you like to see her?' Mum asks again, and her hands move down to my shoulders. 'She looks as if she's sleeping,' she says, and after being sick again, I stand up, my stomach lowering itself hopefully for the last time. Mum wipes my chin with some damp tissue but I still feel like I need to rinse my mouth out, I need to get rid of the taste between my teeth.

She watches me pick up the toothbrush that's been left there for me to use, then hands me a rolled-up toothpaste tube from a cupboard I'm never allowed to open. Then, with no more fruit to carry, together, we walk towards the front room. For the first time in weeks, I'm allowed to push the heavy door open and see who's inside. Nan is lying in the corner. From a distance, it looks as though they were right, that she was just sleeping all this time, yet something feels different. Her flowery duvet is plumped up and draped over her. I want to tuck her in.

'She's not in pain anymore, love, see?' Mum says, and I feel the blood in my face again, my eyes stinging so much that I can't control them. I cry as I see that they've even closed the curtains around the nets, which Nan always thought was too dark. Her face is one that no tangerines can make happy, her smile is missing. I begin to panic that maybe she doesn't even realise she's gone and I want to open the curtains.

I hold onto Nan's hand as tightly as I can, closing my eyes and squeezing her skin and bones together in a way that I hope will make her at least try to wriggle them free. She doesn't, and the skin of her fingers looks shrivelled as though she's been in the bath too long. The room is cold around us and I'm not sure I want to be a grown up anymore if it feels like this. As I wait, Mum holds my other hand and I sense the heat running through the three of us. I open my eyes and taste the salt before it takes its time to roll away.

Diary of a Waste Land

8th May 2013

You'd have been proud of me this morning, David. I finally felt the need to step outside. I began removing the world's rubbish by combing any signs of filth from the forest hair that surrounds our home, then storing it in the unfathomable pockets of my wax jacket. I can hear you now, 'you've lost weight, Pamela. That coat's drowning you,' but at least I'm lighter on my feet for all the walking I intend to do, which surely, can only be a good thing. My very first find was a glass bottle buried in the mud. It was filled with a golden liquid, but don't worry, when I emptied it, there was only the aroma of elderflower cordial.

9th May 2013

Today, I was much more prepared. I carried a black bin liner with me and filled it with litter as often as I could. It's always the bottles that stand out, like half-empty people drowning in the earth. The plastic ones bounced into my bag, misshaping it more each time and it's a good job I shook every dreg away because I found a little creature living inside one of them! The poor thing was a snail, which by the look of its trail, had been slithering up and down the cylinder for a lifetime. I didn't want to frighten it by forcing it out with my fingers, so I tilted the bottle and waited many minutes (you know I've always been patient) for the creature to follow the drops of ginger ale. Well, when it eventually latched onto my palm, I saw just how beautiful it was, the spiral of its shell just eye-rolling at me as it ever-so-slowly glided up the

71

bark alongside us. You once told me (didn't you?) that they sometimes hoist other snails up onto the back of their shells. Well, I wish there had been another one here, so it would've been able to do that.

Anyhow, after walking for an hour or so, I could hardly lug the bag around; it was almost the size of me, so I had no choice but to wrap my arms right around the waist of it, trying my best not to tip the both of us over. I couldn't see anything, mind you, so me and the bin bag had to get used to toppling through the woods in order to get back home safely for the night. As soon as we did return, I dumped the bag alongside the stack of empty plant pots you left around the back of the house, then came up here to have a well-deserved rest, hoping not to dream at all.

10th May 2013

I know nothing would have stopped you, David, but since it rained all this afternoon, I stayed in and began to sort through the rubbish I'd so far unearthed; washing the plastic and rinsing the wrappers, working out what needed to be recycled and what didn't. It took me quite a few hours but it was definitely worth it; very interesting! Mind you, I didn't realise it was such a fertile environment; I found so much contraception lying around the roots of trees like deflated balloons after a birthday party, which reminds me, I really need to wear a safer pair of gloves if I'm going to uncover that sort of thing. I suppose it's good news that people are using it, apart from the unopened packet I stumbled upon; the little, red square was glistening amidst the trodden leaves but I thought I'd better leave it where it was, just in case.

11th May 2013

I'm still sorting through the rubbish, gloves and all! I don't think I'll bother with one of those litter pickers, I find them as fickle as chopsticks, the way they let everything drop from their grasp. I can claw at the dirt better with my own hands as long as this old, grey hair of mine isn't falling in front of my face; I need to get back into the habit of scraping it into my 'headmistress bun,' as you'd have called it.

I found a letter today, stamped but clearly never sent. It was concealed in its own bag of rubbish and I couldn't help but read it when I got home; I'm sure anyone would have, wouldn't they? I assumed it couldn't have been very important if it had been discarded in such a way! It's dated three years ago, so I can't imagine how it got there, but then again, how did anything get there? Once I'd read it, I squeezed it into a new envelope (the old one was so muddy, anyhow) and now I'm trying to decide whether I should forward it on or whether I should leave it be. It's a man called Peter who's pursuing a marriage; he sounds as old as me but the relationship seems very romantic and he was very determined. It's quite sad, he says he wishes life was different but he has no way of changing it. Anyhow, for all I know, it's no more important than all the receipts I've read, all rolled up in the centre of the countryside like little cigarettes.

12th May 2013

Today, I ventured further. I crossed the field of lambs, and then headed towards the woodlands where we used to walk. It was that smell that drew me in the right direction; wild garlic is already in the air again; I saw its long leaves amongst the bluebells. Remember when we brought some home with us? Just the thought makes my stomach growl, but don't worry, I'm currently warming some chicken soup on the stove.

So it was such a shame when my walk was interrupted by a picture from *The Eclipse* newspaper staring up at me from beneath my wellies. It was Page 6, and you know how strongly I feel about that sort of thing. To be honest, it was difficult not to tread it even deeper into the boggy ground when I first noticed the bare breasts

73

presented by a girl whose face I obviously didn't recognise. The sensible side of me insisted that I should put it in the green bag for paper, even though it seemed more appropriate for the bubblegum pink bag intended for plastics. It was just so difficult to consider such an image as biodegradable, David.

By the way, I ended up posting that letter. I certainly wasn't going to place it in the same bag as Page 6. I'm still not sure whether it was the right thing to do. What if it wasn't supposed to be seen? People often write things and show absolutely no one, so perhaps it was none of my business to send it. Then again, it was stamped... You'd be telling me off for meddling, wouldn't you, David? Well, I even wrote my name and address on the back!

13th May 2013

I've been quite enjoying all this clearing up. It's frightening that I ever thought the world was tidy. I've been waking at seven o' clock and walking for two hours, then picking up everything I see on my way back, whether it's been squashed into the ground or blown upwards to nestle on a tree branch. I manage to walk quite a distance in two hours; the ache in my thighs feels good though, it reminds me of our after-lunch Sunday walks.

You'd be happy to hear that the birds were up especially early this morning. A small choir of them were singing their little hearts out in the trees above me, so I had no choice but to wake up earlier for my ramble. At first, it was wonderful, the true essence of spring, I suppose, but it soon became so piercing that I almost went home again. They seemed to want my rubbish, the way they kept pecking around me, not that my finds would have been particularly useful to them. I've managed to see a lot so far; the world is unfortunately decorated by mess, so I should probably be glad I have all this extra time on my hands.

I hope you don't mind but I thought it was time to take the sympathy cards down, so I added them to the rest of the recycling. They're not something I'll want to look back at, but you'd be touched by how many we received from our old students; those children are all grown up now, they have their own families to be thinking about...

Where do dead birds go? I wonder.

14th May 2013

Lately, I've been considering what the word 'waste' actually means. I've always thought of it as something that *was* something or that could still *be* something. I do wonder whether I should be spending all this time litter picking but when I see the difference I've made.... This morning, for example, it's definitely worth it. You were always getting angry about the amount of rubbish people abandoned in the woods, remember, David? Well, now it looks like a little Eden.

Anyhow, after such a successful morning, I headed back out before it became too dark. It's not the sort of place you expect to see many people but I did bump into a man walking a dog. We both nodded and said hello as we crossed paths. He smiled with what seemed to be approval of what I was doing and I smiled back but when I looked again, I saw the dog crouching at the side of the path I'd just cleared, doing its business! I do hope the man picked it up. A little further on, I spotted a young couple entangled beneath a tree. They were so close that at first I thought it was just one person, their laughter was swapping back and forth as easily as breath. That feeling made me want to return to our little cottage. You always held my hand no matter how old we were.

I do hope that letter doesn't cause any bother.

I shouldn't have gone out today. The morning's walk went well because to be honest with you, I've already cleared most of the waste away, but that's why I thought I ought to take advantage of these lighter nights and delve much deeper into the woods. Now, David, I'm all out of sorts.

It all started to go wrong when I almost trod upon a scatter of dried up eggshells. They were pale blue with olive-brown spots. If that isn't the definition of waste, I don't know what is. I was hoping a cuckoo wasn't the culprit because they do that, don't they? Hatch in another bird's nest, and then push the others out? When I looked up, I could see a large nest, high up in the trees; maybe it belonged to magpies. Then, just a little further on, I discovered something dreadful. I really shouldn't have delved.

It was the smell that first overwhelmed me, like the meaty insides of a butcher's shop, or an animal longer-dead than that, perhaps at the stage where it has to be dumped. I was searching behind the trees, expecting to find the usual tissues, maybe some crisp packets or cigarette boxes, and then there in front of me was the source of that repulsive odour and I couldn't have imagined anything worse; it was a person lying dead in the damp mud! The stench was definitely the worst, so thick that it seemed to creep up my nose and right into me. Every time I tried to breathe in, it made me feel so light-headed that I was afraid to stay any longer in case I collapsed upon it, its long, straggly hair draping over us both. What were left of its eyes had been picked at from two, bloody hollows and its chest was so bony it had lost all definition. I couldn't help but scramble away as soon as possible. When I was finally at home, I picked up the phone and told the police where the body was. I think I need to lie down but I'm afraid the poor body will give me nightmares. Do you think something brutal happened to it, David? Either way, I know I'll never erase that sight from my mind.

The police asked many questions, though I know I shouldn't have expected anything less. I had to lead them towards the site where I'd found the body and I was glad they drove us most of the way; I've done so much walking recently. They said it was an unusual place to be walking around, alone, at that time of evening and asked if my family worried about me and I told them you would, if you hadn't passed away two months ago. Then they said they understood that I was coping with a lot, lately. It is a lot, David. I told them about all the litter I've collected and I was sure I saw a magpie swoop over the policeman's head but it disappeared as I saluted it. That was the moment they found the body in the dip behind the trees. They use the largest of cameras and the smallest of notepads.

They told me they were eternally grateful.

'Now, we need you to step away from the area,' they said.

I told them there was no need to be grateful because I've been clearing the area for a week. I'm just glad to have been of some use.

Just now, I looked up where dead birds go. If they aren't eaten, they rapidly wither away.

22nd May 2013

This past week, I've been glad to hear the bird song again. I cleaned the outside of the house as much as I possibly could. You know I'm not usually the one to do it, so I didn't realise how much hard work it would be, all that weeding and hosing down of the patio, tidying up the flower borders – you usually take the rubbish out too, all whilst listening to your radio outside, always the same station with those distinctive, authoritative voices.

At the moment, it's light at nine o' clock, so I've had the chance to make up for what I've missed and head back into the wild. Luckily, it didn't look as though there was much change in terms of mess, so I needn't have worried so much. Of course, I avoided the area where the police had assembled and instead, headed into the thick of the forest.

23rd May 2013

I received a phone call from the police today. I was worried, I didn't want it to be a never-ending process. They asked if I still had any of the litter remaining from the recent weeks, from around the area where the body had been found. I told them that I do but also explained why it's taking me a very long time to sort through it. I haven't been sleeping very well, you see, so I've been feeling quite fatigued. There are three bags left and I've missed the recycling men. It's safe to say that finding the body has had its effects on me. I told the police they could feel free to take it off my hands in the morning, as long as they were certain it wouldn't end up making a mess of the countryside again. This week has worn me out.

24th May 2013

When I answered the phone this evening, a detective informed me,
'The body you found was that of a young girl.'
Apparently, it was a girl who's been missing and searched for, for over six months. When he said it, my heart seemed to draw right up inside my chest. I started to imagine the thankful but sad eyes of the family; maybe my interference had somewhat helped? The girl had overdosed on heroin and they'd found a syringe in my rubbish! Honestly, David, the things our little cottage has witnessed these past few weeks… I could have done with my litter picker in that case. The detective said it was unsuspected and explained how it's brought the case to a close, even though it's an unfortunate ending. He told me again, how grateful they all are for my help, but it wasn't help, I was just doing my job.
Then he said that one of my newspapers had her picture on it and the word 'Missing' printed above it.

'It was in *The Eclipse*,' he said. Can you believe it?

Well, you know I've never read that, but it's good to know that paper runs at least some important news. Anyhow, he didn't say anymore, so I said he could pass on my contact details to the girl's family, just in case they ever want to speak to me, more for their reasons than my own.

21st December 2013

It's been months since I began my new hobby, my new job, cleaning up this waste land of a countryside. I haven't received any phone calls concerning the young girl's body but I suppose I did intrude upon something tragic, something private, even if it was entirely unintentional. I'm just glad they were able to put her to rest.

I looked up the accurate definition of 'waste' in the dictionary this afternoon.

The top results were:

'Use or expend carelessly, extravagantly, or to no purpose:'

'Fail to make full or good use of:'

I think I'll walk somewhere new tomorrow. What do you think, David?

22nd December 2013

I've been feeling so lonely at home these past few days, David. It doesn't help that it's bitterly cold outside, so my walking hasn't gone to plan at all. Christmas has crept into the air too, which certainly doesn't help matters; I was hoping it would glide over our cottage this year. I've been able to sense it since the clocks went back; the night time approaches so early that it's impossible to do anything but go home or stay home. I've been trying to sleep more but time just seems to stretch ahead of me like one bin liner after another and I only wake up in the dark again.

I was so glad when the phone rang today; it's been a while since I heard that nightingale ringtone, you know, the one you chose. It woke me right up from a nightmare and it took me a few seconds before I finally realised I wasn't in the woods with birds pecking at me, but on the sofa!

I didn't recognise the lady's voice when I answered. If anything, I assumed it was a wrong number but the lady asked if a Pamela lived here! I panicked then, you know me, I'd never considered they would *actually* call about the body, I assumed all that had been dealt with.

I must have sounded worried when I asked who was calling because the lady felt the need to say she didn't want to alarm anyone. Then she explained how she hoped I didn't mind, and she knew it had been a while but it *is* Christmas, so she looked up my name in the directory from a return address I'd included on a letter I sent a few months back. I couldn't remember having written any letters, not for years! My silly memory is forgetting all the little things.

Anyhow, she said she was Caroline, the very lady from the letter! I was panicking even more when she said that because there are always repercussions, aren't there? The way she said, 'You must have found it somewhere near where we used to live,' made me feel guilty. My chest felt so tight that I realised I hadn't been breathing, but when she said how thankful she was, I let out a long breath into the handset. She explained that her husband, Peter, died a year after writing that letter, but they got back together before the end. She said it all worked out! Aren't you glad to hear that? Apparently, Peter was very ill and that was why there was a temporary break between them in the first place. She'd always wondered why he ended it that time and with him being so ill afterwards, they never had a chance to discuss it, so thanks to me, she finally knew. Can you believe it? I can hear her words now, as if she's still saying them, 'Do you realise how it feels to read his words when I never thought I'd hear from him ever again? It's like he's speaking to me from another world. I finally know he never stopped loving me, not for a second!' She could probably tell from my voice that I was smiling as I spoke.

I'm still smiling now! I feel excited for her, for everything. At first, I laughed out loud and then, I of course told the lady how happy I was to hear that their time together was spent well and how relieved I was to have not caused any problems. She even suggested that we meet up for a coffee in the new year. What do you think, David? Should I?

Since hanging up, I feel as though I could hear about a story like that forever. It's made me feel like my veins are bubbling, like I can do anything for anyone and I want to tell you about it properly, David, if only you could speak to me too. Yet, all I feel able to do at the moment, is sit upright on the sofa with everything around me. It's so silent and I can't remember the last time I felt this overwhelmed. I want to celebrate by opening one of your old bottles of rum. You said you were saving it for something special, didn't you? I'm sure I can hear you if I really try. Can you speak through china walls? From the dust? Have you settled?

'Treat yourself, darling,' you'd say. Your voice is clear, as though you're the one the other end of the line, cheerful but blunt. 'You're always doing more for others than for yourself,' you'd say, and I know I'm rolling my eyes but this hobby of mine has helped me so much.

I haven't stopped thinking about what waste means.
'Fail to make full or good use of:'
Fail to make full or good use of it...
That's it. I'm in the practise of sorting what isn't of good use, and tomorrow, I may try to sort through your old clothes. You won't

mind, will you? It just feels like you aren't in them anymore. When I hear you, I can see you but I can't touch you and I need to get used to that. I won't get rid of your photographs of the birds because I might even learn something. I'll find the one of the cuckoo that you Blu-tacked next to the clock before I said how much I hated it, but it was because you told me what they do, remember?

They abandon their own eggs in the nests of other birds. Then a little cuckoo, inside an egg so big, grows up and pushes the others out. I remember saying how selfish they were and you just laughed, pointing at its stocky stance, ready to bulldoze through life. Do you remember? I can hear you laughing now. I'll have another look at it; maybe I'll hear the up and down of its call, prodding at me, *cuckoo, cuckoo*. In fact, I'll frame the culprit above the clock, so its stocky body sits above the constant tick. I think that would be a very good idea.

Turnstones

I used to wonder what my world looked like from above; whether people would notice if one of us disappeared or whether I could just fly away and settle somewhere else. I used to think they could easily replace me with a stone, just something to bridge the gap between the moss of colour, if that's all I was, just a fleck of a painting, something to fill the white wind in wintery months. But no one else around here seems to consider it, or at least they don't talk about it. I've always been told to hush up every time I ask any questions and to carry on eating. Mother said I should be grateful for such a beautiful Swansea coast and I know she's right, but it's easy to take things for granted after a while.

Here, there is plenty of fresh air to breathe in and in and in, but there isn't enough space to breathe it all back out again. There are about a hundred just like me, all packed together, and with their bright, orange legs, treading on my territory, just as I'm treading on theirs. Although, I should emphasise how we're all a little different, that's what people forget, they aren't really me at all. We each have a different number of brown and black speckles and some of us have much cleaner white bellies than others, with bigger black bibs around our necks and chests. That's how we distinguish each other during our sea-feasts together, where we probe the sand – beak after beak – for whatever we can find, clicking with a *kitititit kitititit* as we discover sloppy worms or fly larvae to gulp down before the meal is over. I remember the first time I saw Father and how he taught me to gather food. He flipped over a stone the size of his own body and I was impressed

83

by such steady, yet intricate strength, never truly seeing myself in his position. Of course, the very same day, that's exactly what I was doing; flipping over stones, sticks and runny moss all morning and afternoon, discovering all sorts of worms and molluscs underneath.

I make a special effort to remember everything I find, whether it's from beneath a stone or not. It helps to give me a sense of the surroundings. If the object is edible, all the more reason for me to try and remember it. Most of the time, it's one of the crusts of bread people throw over the sea wall to us, or a salty chip from the hole-in-the-wall café. Mother said the bread is bad for our stomachs, yet last time it happened, I saw her eyes on the crumbs as soon as they started tumbling through the air towards us; I'm sure that's why she attempted to put us off. It usually happens when people are walking across the promenade; they'll be having a conversation and then all of a sudden, a whole slice comes flying our way and we have to duck before it lands in an appropriate place where we all squabble over it. For a long time, I wasn't sure about those people the other side of the wall because they were throwing things at us all the time, but Mother informed me that we should be very grateful for the food they provide. Sometimes, I see them peeping over and playing games with us and they don't ask permission, so then I *really* play games with them. When I hear them say, 'try and spot the turnstones,' I breathe in and in and in and stay still for as long as I possibly can. They think we know nothing.

I've flown a lot, but still not as often as I'd like. Whenever I've soared over the world below, I've imagined myself transforming into something different: one of the bright red balloons little children let go of and cry over; one of the scary, toothy dogs on leads, similar to the kind in the Arctic; or one of the fleshy people who wade through the blue all around us. It's the blue that intrigues me the most. Recently, I flew right down onto the face of a person wading in it whilst their eyes were closed, but I had to hop back up into the air before they blinked them open again. Mother said not to delve too deeply into the blue, she said the less I know, the better and that I should keep to the shore, but I'd like to stand out from the rest. I have these wings and yet I haven't been able to use them enough. It upsets me that people can so easily mistake us for soggy moss or black pebbles but Mother said it can also be a blessing that we blend in so well, so the falcons don't get us. I know she's right, but it feels like there may be more out there, more to explore. That's why I get so side-tracked by playing with the visitors, messing with their minds.

Last time I did this, a tiny body was peeping over the coastal wall and it assumed it was staring at perfectly still ground. When I could tell it felt at ease, I shuffled to the left, which flipped over a stone next to me, in turn flipping over my sister who was standing upon it; *she* fell on the edge of another stone, which in turn flipped over a cousin of ours and a turnstone earthquake had been caused all by me, presenting a turnstone at its best. First there was a *kitititit kitititit* and then there was a *i i i i i i i i i i* from every turnstone including myself. The eyes of the body at the wall kept blinking and blinking as though it doubted what it was witnessing, its mouth gasping open, then closed, its face looking unsettled, having initially thought we were nothing but a pile of stones along the water's edge. Eventually, it walked away.

There's a lot we don't talk about. The most recent topic is the person we discovered many months back. At first, it looked just like the people we often see wading when we're closer to the bay, but it seemed to become bigger and bigger, its head clearly larger than one of us. It floated as a whole solid towards us, its legs not moving individually as usual, but just allowing the deep to carry it forward. Then it stopped. It quivered a little as five of its fingers knocked against the stones near my left. It shook one stone, so the one above tumbled and I rolled from where I was perched,

right onto the chest of the person. I could hear an *i i i i i i i i i i*
and panicked until I realised it was coming from my own beak.
Then I looked at Mother, her beak opening and closing with a
Pri pri pri pri pri pri as I paced back and forth over the person's
chest, afraid of what it would do to me. After a while, I realised
it wasn't going to do anything at all. This seemed strange but
Mother put a stop to me asking anymore questions.

Mother's hush ups have always encouraged my inquisitive
nature, so I stared at the decaying lump of flesh before us all, its
eyes so tightly closed that I could tap my feet across them. I
wondered where it had floated from and if anyone had noticed
if this body was missing, since it was much too large to have lived
under a stone. I felt agitated when interrupted by my Mother,
who was working her way down the layers of stones towards me,
then landing on one of the person's legs. This led my brothers
and sisters to follow in her footsteps before cousin after cousin
joined in, hustling all of us around the still body, all bewildered
by the pinkish grey oddity.

Standing there, I became aware of something that made me
feel uneasy, something that began to tug at my stomach: the fact
that it was me who was standing at the centre of this washed-up
giant, where there should have been a heartbeat nudging me
away, something other than the blue's gentle waves washing over
our backs. The peculiar feeling increased when we began to peck
away at it as though it was just another worm. I wondered if
perhaps I was witnessing our painting changing, different colours
being splashed on, then nibbled away by our very own gobbling
beaks. We were pecking one by one, then together, then with no
pattern at all, just fiercely pecking between speckled stones along
the stony part of the coast that, from above, must have appeared
to swirl and swirl in black and brown and white flecks.

It provided me with new things to consider in my coastal home.
I stared at the pink mound of flesh again. It was beginning to

scatter in a greyed fuchsia between us and I wondered how many of us it would take to replace it. Moments before, it had resembled one of the people who had waded close to the bay, like the one whose head I had landed upon. I saw Mother pecking, pecking, pecking; saw my sisters pecking, pecking, pecking; heard the *kitititit kitititit* and my stomach tugged again. I couldn't seem to entirely block it out; it was similar to when I ate the tiny eggs Mother sometimes found and shared between us. Something feels strange about them, when they're rotating around my mouth, in the same way it felt strange that we were pecking and ripping away at the shrivelled skin of the giant. I remember stepping back and seeing us cover it in our moss of colour, burying it beneath our bodies, blending it into the painting with our feet, so it gradually became smaller. I remember looking into Mother's eyes again, but she told me to carry on.

Mother froze and began to lie low and at first I wasn't sure why, but then I saw she was trying to camouflage herself against what remained of the person's chest beneath her. I could see there was a problem with her black and white body standing out against the swollen pink. The others followed suit and I ducked down to the edge of the stones I was resting against, peeping up whenever I found the courage. There was a large bird hovering above us all, one I hadn't seen before, but it appeared like one Mother had once described: the falcon. All of a sudden, it folded its wings and dived down, catching Mother in its half-open claw and stealing her away. I could hear her voice calling to me with a *pri pri pri pri*, but it became fainter as she became more distant. I wondered where she was being taken and what our painting looked like to her from above, as she soared through the sky at a speed she would have never experienced before. I watched her until she became a dot and then nothing. I wondered if she was planning to settle somewhere and whether she would come back, but something told me that she wouldn't and it tugged at my stomach more horribly than when I had eaten those tiny eggs or pecked away at the flesh in front of me.

For moments afterwards, there was a thick silence surrounding us all; nothing but the blue, sounding more terrifying than it ever had. Then I began calling back to Mother, just in case she could hear. *i i i i i, i i i i i,* I called, *i i i i i, i i i i i,* so the others joined in, one and then the next, our beaks pointing up to the sky as high as we could lift them, all of us standing in a cluster but one of us missing. Hearing the echo of our high-pitched family merging together from sister to brother and from cousin to cousin and turning our backs to the sea wall to hear more clearly, I felt my body stiffen, then my head slump towards my feet. Something told me we wouldn't be able to replace Mother with a stone; something told me we wouldn't be able to replace her with anything we found.

Confidence Class

I opened the wardrobe door and found her sitting there, buried amongst the clothes. Not in the way a coat sometimes comes alive in the darkness or a clock smiles at specific times, but two legs folded up like an ironing board and the knobbly faces of two knees wrapped in a pair of very elbowed arms. A second look and I could see a chin dribbling old tears down my striped, chiffon skirt. I struggled to push it to one side but the hanger didn't budge. Then, as a nose poked out from between the moth-scented material and I pulled the skirt free, the girl's little fists were climbing across it and twisting it into a silky stick of rock. Behind it, in the dark space, other skirts spread like Spanish fans and two eyes were revealed: mine, looking back at me, but with a thick layer of sadness resting over the irises. As I blinked, so did she, her lids spilling tears over her cheekbones. I watched them run into the tufts of soggy hair in front of her ears.

She was young and dainty enough to sit on the shelf of my wardrobe, and her skin was pale against such black hair, which was so poker-straight that it caused the long fringe to split over her eyebrows. It was difficult not to notice the veins tinselled into the bags beneath her eyes. For a few minutes, it was almost as though she had forgotten to cry and then she would rush to catch up with three breaths all at once, her chest uncontrollably pumping, making it impossible for her to remain silent. The longer I stared, the calmer she became, and her desperate struggle for breath grew more gradual. She looked back at me, helplessly, as though one word or one touch could push her over the edge.

I was only halfway through the autumn term at uni, so I really didn't need this, I needed to be on time. I rifled through the possible clothing options for that day and as usual, it was to be a bright choice; a green polo neck with brown, tartan shorts and thick, orange tights. I always felt better when surrounded by colour, whereas the little girl seemed to sulk in greys and blacks. She draped one of my long cardigans around her like a blanket, using the sleeve to wipe her nose. When I peeled it away, her hand clutched onto the leg of my shorts, and her eyes, which had been screwed up tight, looked up at me again, growing bigger and bigger as though she was pleading with me to help her. I looked back at her, concerned about what she expected from me.

'What's wrong?' I asked, but she insisted on burying her face in her folded arms, her whole body beginning to shake so much, I was afraid she might crumble into dust all over the clothes around her. I began to wonder how much crying such a small body could do, but it seemed to continue bursting with sadness so overwhelming, she couldn't contain herself. Then something ambled out of her mouth: a single 'I.' That was all she said, though she mumbled it several times between rushed breaths and exhaled heavily after each one, sobbing more relentlessly and knocking upon air as though it was another door she wanted to push open.

'I? Yes, I?' I asked, probing for something more.

'Yes,' she said, nodding fast as though her head was upon a tiny spring. There was that look again, that helpless, hopeless look, which brought a dark and unsettling sensation throughout my body. Confused, I pointed to myself and she nodded, throwing one leg down from under her chin. The other followed, levering her onto the carpet. When I walked, she followed and I allowed her to.

She was too sad and impossible to let go of. It had been a few months since she'd begun following me: she sat in my car;

traipsed behind me along the university corridors and came to the lectures I was able to attend; she had become a shadow, which had to be dragged along and I felt a sense of guilt whenever I acknowledged how I truly felt; that I wished I'd never met her that morning in the wardrobe. I didn't like her, and the guiltier her neglected face made me feel, the closer to hating her I became. Deep down, in the pit of her misery, she must have known because sometimes, she would quickly glance at me and catch me gritting my teeth as I tried not to curse out loud. That's when she used to grasp my hand so tightly that my fingers would crunch together; she would even interrupt important conversations and lead me away from social gatherings. She was very strong, in her own way and I would dread her warning whimper, a low octave of only three notes, *boo-hoo-hoo, boo-hoo-hoo*. That's when I knew we would have to escape before this transformed into an awkwardly melodramatic episode.

It always began with a trembling of the hands, a protruding of the bottom lip and then the girl's chest would rise and fall rapidly out of control, her mouth opening and closing as though it belonged to a little fish gasping for air. At first, she would shy away from me, hiding her face so emphatically that it only brought more attention to the two eyes staring through her fingers. Then those gaps would begin to leak with sadness, which I couldn't help but taste to be every flavour of morbidity spilling over me and sinking into the ground where we both stood. She would try to absorb the cries in her little, pink hands, but there were too many, especially when her nose would start to run, her face spouting like a solemn water feature.

The little girl's hands were always so wet from tears that they made my palms clammy when she grabbed hold of them and we would rush out of the room. We always went to the same place, the toilets, our comforting sanctuary where no one else could intervene, where no one else had to deal with her outbursts but me. That's when the dark wave would ebb away and she would smile, her mouth spreading slightly at the corners, not happy, but as though something was temporarily resolved. Of course, the atmosphere was always awful; full of self-punishing talks and apologies.

With no other options, I decided to take her along to a Confidence Class. There had been posters around the university stating that everyone was welcome. She'd become so settled in my wardrobe that sometimes, I could hardly find her behind the layers of clothing; she was so wrapped up in herself. Eventually, I saw her little body curled up in the centre of a hammock she had created from long dresses that flowed across the wardrobe. I poked her, but she wouldn't come out, so I had to lift her out with both hands and even then, she just stood outside the glass door, hunched over at the shoulders, skinny and doe-eyed. She was like a child who needed to be coaxed. I had to hide outside the bedroom door, pretending I had left her alone in order for her to tread after me. It was the first occasion that I had particularly wanted her company. It was more about her than me, you see; about her soggy face and the way it ducked behind her knees.

It was when we finally walked into the Confidence Class that it was confirmed: she was one of them and I was not: one of the circle of sadness before us, sitting in frozen shapes, each one of them hunched at the shoulders, their heads drooping and threatening to fall off like those of wilting flowers and their eyes afraid to peer out. One by one, we were instructed to speak about how we felt, so when it was my turn, I let the little girl speak instead. Sat on the floor beside my chair, she uncurled herself and I witnessed her mouth opening and her body tensing. I smiled at her and nodded.

'Go on,' I whispered. 'Go on.'

'I,' she mumbled. 'I.' Then she turned and spoke more loudly to everyone in the circle, just saying 'I,' over and over again and opening her big, round eyes to look up at me. If I didn't know her better, I would have assumed it to be a stammer, but I knew her much more than I had ever intended.

'I?' I asked, pointing at myself, playing her little game, feeling that dark sensation spread over me again, when everyone turned and looked in my direction. Then she nodded, whispering in my ear,

'Tell them how I make you feel,' and I swear I could feel the coldness of her breath on the side of my neck. She looked at me more sadly then, beginning to whimper *boo-hoo-hoo, boo-hoo-hoo*, her words spreading out between pauses and rushes of collected breath. It was almost too much to handle. The image of her sobbing in my wardrobe was haunting me; the little girl, always inside.

I sat up and cleared my throat.

'I,' I began, perhaps with a slight stammer whilst trying to straighten my back. 'I feel as though,' my chin sank downwards. Even though I couldn't see the little girl anymore, I could feel the nod of her head trying to maintain the momentum of my sentence and I couldn't give up. I took a deep breath. 'I feel as though I was created by mistake.' I said it clearly and honestly, surprised by the sound of my own voice gathering itself from somewhere deep down in a place I hadn't yet discovered, a place filled with words ready to flutter out of my mouth at any given moment if I willed them to wake up. I opened my eyes and around me was a circle of synchronised nods. I heard the little girl's snivelling, but like the count between rolls of thunder, each groan was further away. She wiped her nose with the back of her hand and a strange smile seemed to spread across her face. Then she used her knees to push up onto standing feet, leaving me alone in a room full of strangers, with a silence begging to be filled.

Nostalgia

Neave picks a flower called Nostalgia from the garden wall. Shortly after, she tries to slot it back into the bunch. She'd assumed it would be as easy as a pin cushion, the leaves minding space for the spike of the Nostalgia's stem, but when she speaks to it and consoles its green, withering limb with her thumb, it only faints towards the concrete.

'There's no such thing as a Nostalgia.'

That's what David says. He's hurling a tennis ball at the wall of their house, hitting the same, red brick, over and over again. Every time it bounces back, he catches it with a firm claw, swapping between left and right.

'Like *you* would know.' Neave's already rescued the flower and is holding it beneath her chin. She closes her eyes and inhales until her head feels dizzy. If this was a movie, she'd be transported straight to somewhere better.

Instead, a sneeze catapults her back, the corners of her eyelids pinching open to the sun. If she properly angles her hand above her brow, she can just about see her mother on the other side of this green rectangle; a skirt of sunlight around her as though she's magically emerging from the ground.

Neave's seen her mother like this plenty of times, a constant flicker in their large and rectangular garden; she's usually relocating bird baths or shuffling a rockery around, but lately, something's different. Neave can hear the double-beat of the ball hitting the wall, then leaving; *thu-dump, thu-dump, thu-dump,* as the smooth muscles in her mother's shoulders roll back and forth

95

and she rests upon her green knees. Lately, her mother hasn't been eager to converse. Instead, she sometimes pauses and rests her gentle hand upon the turf she re-laid a few weeks ago, only a few footsteps away from the new hole she's digging, then carries on.

'Sorry, love. No such thing as a Nostalgia.' This is the first time in a long time that she has intervened. As soon as she's said it, her hand drops back into the earth.

'What's this, then?' Neave asks. She's stretching her arm out as far as it will go and holding the flower against the sky. If she squints, its buttermilk flurry looks just like the sun.

'That's a Nasturtium.' Neave's brother is already laughing.

'It's a lovely name,' Neave says, even though she can see how busy her mother is, removing rocks from the soil, then placing them in a little heap alongside the depression in the earth.

'It's a *lovely* name.' Her brother's high pitch and grin make Neave annoyed.

'Stop it!' As he grins again, the tennis ball springs back from the wall and pelts the side of his face until it crinkles up.

'Where did you hear about Nostalgia?' asks Neave's mum.

'I saw it on Dad's gardening programme!' Neave's mother still doesn't look as though she's paying attention; her ashy ponytail just sweeps back and forth.

'But a Nostalgia isn't a flow—'

'I saw it,' Neave says, 'I promise I saw it on the telly! The man with the white, rice pudding-hair said it.'

'You must be mixing things up—'

'He told us about a holiday he went on with his family. There was a cottage and a lot of walks and he said his legs used to ache but it was worth it. He said they went to the same cottage every year and whatever month it was, he'd see the yellow flowers. Then he said, "*this* is Nostalgia." Mam, why are you smiling?'

Neave's mother is considering their usual holidays. Last summer, they went to Cornwall in their caravan. Her husband

96

always thought it was best to keep moving; that's why he taught the children to ride bikes without stabilisers before they could swim. *These days, you ll get further on road than in water,* he'd say, and she couldn't argue with something that was probably true, even though the caravan was sat on its rusty behind for most of the year, which she supposes children never realise.

Her daughter's eyes are closed again. She is starting to remind her of a doll she had when she was a little girl; it had lids that snapped open and shut whenever it was moved. On one occasion, she'd shook it so much that the left eye never wholly opened again but only teetered halfway as though it was swollen or asleep. Her daughter, on the other hand, has the animated face of her father, whose round eyes could never keep still. Even through the lids, she can see Neave's flickerings, and she never dares to interrupt, doesn't dare to make them still.

Instead, she wonders how to explain nostalgia to someone so small, whose past hardly exists. Her own would involve this garden, this house, this city, this country and further, since they'd had the caravan. All she has to do is catch a reflection of herself and she sees her husband's view of her, or she moves in a certain way and she feels the outline of her chest, its fault-lines ready to quake underneath.

As she looks across to the cluster of yellow flowers on the wall above Neave's head, she wonders if the neighbours the other side have guessed anything. She was irritated weeks ago when she saw someone pressed up against the window, probably watching her at work with two arms, rather than the usual four. Never mind, she hears her son laughing again because a lime green ball is flying through the air towards her daughter. David's always laughing at the wrong things.

'David!' She's never been able to take her stern voice seriously. 'Fetch me the lawnmower from the shed, will you?' She can feel her back aching as it straightens. She's decided that

97

she's left the subject for long enough. 'Neave, it was nostalgia to the man, but it's not Nostalgia to us.' As her son drags his feet past her, she notices that his hair is much darker lately, more like hers, whereas Neave's has so far remained a curious, Nordic blonde.

Regardless of suffering a blow to the back, Neave is as usual, unfazed. One more try, Neave thinks, again attempting to return the flower to its original display. The leaves have white spokes that make them look like tiny umbrellas, or parachutes for when they dive from the wall.

'I don't get it.' The Nostalgia only sticks for a second, then flops, no parachute in tow.

Her mother considers leaving the conversation there. Would it really hurt not to explain? Her daughter is smiling just like she did when she was three years old and she was presented with her very first doll: she'd combed its hair over and over for two days straight, amazed by the shine, but once satisfied, never picked it up again. The doll sits on the top of her wardrobe, wearing a hat of dust; perhaps this would be the same.

'Neave, that flower means a lot to the man on TV for specific reasons.' Her daughter is already looking at it differently, her grip loosening. 'Not the one you're holding, just that kind of flower. See how many there are?' She notices those round eyes absorbing the tens of Nasturtiums along the wall. This feels like the time she told her how Father Christmas doesn't exist in the way everyone says he does, or when she told David to continue asking as many questions as he wanted to at his RE class because there's no real truth. He eventually stopped asking.

She tries again. 'The man associates that flower with happy memories. So every time he sees or smells it, all those pleasant times come flooding back and he wants to return to them. That's what nostalgia is; the feeling he has whenever he's around the flower.'

'Really?' Neave asks. She's trying not to hold the flower so tightly when she realises the stem is threatening to snap but she's also decided not to let go of it ever again.

Her eyes blink another snapshot of the Nasturtiums. There's too much green where she's taken the flower away and she doesn't like it; it reminds her of the time she spilled water all over a painting a few years before. She'd waited hours for it to dry until she could repaint the ruined section, a little Mallard duck in a large lake. No matter how much paint she used, it never looked the same as it had originally; the duck was just a giant, spectral blur in a loom of water. Dad said he'd sketch the outline of it for her again another time but they ended up framing it as it was.

'Please be careful with those flowers.' Neave jumps, Dad was right; her mother really does notice everything.

'It's the same Nostalgia, I promise!'

'Nasturtium, love.' Her mother doesn't like the way Neave uses the word 'promise' so easily, even if it's the truth. Her mother's voice speaks down to her chest; she's forgotten what she was thinking before. Was it the caravan? No, she's wiping the summer glow away from her face; that's what her husband would call it, but he'd erase any glow just as often. He'd tell her about his other worlds, you know, the places inside his head, the other continents he was so desperate to visit, to feel the burn of sun on his back, to encounter new cultures and experiences without limitation. She should have been glad that he was sharing his dreams aloud but there was something painful about always being the listener and never a partner in his delusion.

It felt a little like being sent a beautifully scenic postcard so many times that you begin to study the gloss of the picture rather than what's in it; the writing style, the way it's signed, how many kisses are written and when concentrating on the stamps, finally realising that you're never the sender but always the recipient.

99

The strangest thing was, after all his talk, he only ended up travelling a few streets away, to explore the contours of another woman's body.

Neave has already become interested in the flower again. She's twirling it around, imagining herself as tiny as Thumbelina and perched in the centre of it. It's just like one of those rides her Dad used to spin them around on in the park a few streets away; the giant spinning tops you have to hang on to. *Around and around and around and around and around and around*, her father used to shout, *faster and faster and faster and faster*, and she'd close her eyes to imagine that somewhere better, even then.

Nasturtium. She whispers it to herself and begins to feel dizzy again. Her mother is smiling but her eyes stay turned towards the ground. Neave looks around at the image of the garden, places her hand above her eyes and blinks as though she's stealing another snapshot. There's her mother, hunched over in the corner, in pale jeans and a vest top that used to be white. Perhaps the flash would alter that, if there was one, but Dad always took the photographs. Her mother's brown shoulders are beginning to wrinkle, probably because she's always pressing the ground as though she's searching for a pulse.

Slightly to the right is her brother David, who's dragging his feet away from a lawn mower he's finally wheeled out onto the grass. Now, he's kicking a ball against the shed door until it rolls back and he kicks it again – again – again. Neave wonders how long he can do this for without saying anything. There's a basketball hoop somewhere; Dad nailed it onto the wall at the side of the house but David won't use it.

'Mam.'

'Yes, love?' Her mother's voice sounds sharper, she's still huffing and puffing.

'Do you think the man would mind sharing his Nostalgia with me?'

Hearing this, her mother's chest feels like it's closing up. Why did Neave have to be so much like her father? It was sweet, inexplicable sentences like this that drew her back *like a river to the sea,* as he'd say. Now, she tries to remember how the stigma of his tongue had sickened her over time.

She notices the earth has been falling through her fingers; she'll have to dig it all out again. She looks around, worried that this will be her daughter's only happy memory, the worst thing being that when she had first told Neave that she would be digging up earth in the garden, Neave had thought she was referring to the actual earth, the entire planet. She was going to correct her on that occasion too, before she realised how her daughter was in a sense, correct. Seeing that smiling face, she knows how she'll have to answer the question; her daughter's world was rotating enough already. She turns to her and says, 'I'm sure the man won't mind sharing his nostalgia at all.'

Neave closes her eyes and sniffs the Nasturtium beneath her nose, so much that the pits of her nostrils itch and she has to rub them with the knuckles of her other hand. She tries to focus, *nostalgia, nostalgia, nostalgia*, but other moments begin to interfere: happy moments, extremely happy, always hot, with thick, yellow light and no breeze or discomfort at all, kind of like being imposed onto the sticky shine of a photograph without enough movement to be a film. There she is, painting again, her legs crossed underneath her before the water spills and ruins it all, creeping across the paper until it all looks like the view through a soppy car window.

Then another. Their dilapidated tent is open upon the lawn and taking up so much space that they're all struggling around it, apart from Neave's mother who is crouched inside after just clipping its roof together. Her dad begins to hose down the walls of it to make sure there are no leaks and as he does, his wife's shadow squeals from the inside, as icy water pierces through the holes. When she finally unzips the door and crawls out, her hair is dripping and her eyes are wide and startled, so she steals the hose and drenches Neave's dad with it. A few months later, the caravan arrives in front of the house, with everything so compact that it never stops surprising them all with its secret compartments.

All four of them are in most of the moments, but when Neave's nose begins to itch even more, the details ink themselves in; all of them have the ability to move but they seem to stay still. The happier Neave feels as she remembers them, the sadder she feels straight afterwards, as though someone is pouring water away as soon as she begins to feel quenched. If she submerged the memories in water, perhaps the colours would run and develop into something better, just as she'd witnessed in movies.

Sometimes, she forgets they had a dog. He was racing around the tent, too. Their dad called it Daft but it wasn't his name. He used to bound across the kitchen as soon as Dad's face could be seen at the door after work and it was Daft's tail that knocked the cup of water over. That's right, Neave had been angry with him for it because it had ruined the painting. She cried for days and didn't stroke Daft the whole time. In fact, it's the only time she can remember her father shouting at her. He was crouching over the dog as if it was a puppy he'd just brought home and pointing his finger, saying, *Accidents happen, Neave, accidents happen!* She even thought she'd seen his eyes filling up.

Neave's eyes are beginning to itch from the Nostalgia in her hand. She's sniffing and her eyes are beginning to stream so much that even when she tries to open them, the thick tears make the image of the garden appear much differently, more like the wet painting. She sneezes again.

'That flower isn't good for you,' her mother says, finally turning around, 'your hay fever must be playing up.' As Neave nods, a sheet of tears falls, so she can't see anything through what has by now, become a soppy window. She runs towards the house with her eyes barely open, feeling as clumsy as the dog as she leaps over the threshold. Inside, she imagines the stairs continuing up and up and up, far away from the humidity and far away from those tiny specks that ruin her vision.

There in her bedroom, is the desk she sits at whenever this happens. Dad set it up years ago, right below the window, so she could look out over everything and paint, or as her mother suggested, make paper flowers. Neave can't believe that paper comes from trees. Looking at the Nostalgia still in her hand, its petals have grown so brittle that their buttery colour is breaking into thick strands. She goes to close the window against the pollen, which is trying to breathe upon her, but she can hear muttering outside. If this was before, it would be both of her parents looking up at her, arms around each other's waists with the sun on their faces.

David's laugh breaks into the image, which his mother uses as an opportunity to ask him for help. Neave sees them planting a large tree into the new hole in the garden. Her mother asks David if he misses their dog but Neave doesn't hear what he mumbles back. She only sees that he chooses not to clamber at the soil any longer but instead turns around and walks towards the house. His mother shouts after him, 'I miss him, too,' but David's already in. Neave shuts the window, and then rushes back to her desk. She can hear the creak of her brother's feet on the stairs and eventually, he opens the door to her room.

Without saying anything, he sits alongside her. Neave notices that his eyes are red and puffy like hers but she doesn't say anything. She passes him one of the long straws she's been pasting petals onto and he continues, knowing what to do, his chunky fingers shaking with concentration as he holds the sugary, paper leaves between them.

Together, they create one flower, then another and another, all in different colours. Whilst her brother is Sellotaping the last one,

Neave looks through the window once again to see what her mother is doing but she's still in the same, crouched position.

'At least these are permanent,' David says, placing another stem into the plastic vase on the windowsill. Neave notices how the tree isn't far from where Daft was buried.

For that memory, Neave sees a bleak day. Nobody is running or laughing and in fact, there are only three of them present. Daft had died the day before; he'd whined for weeks after Dad left, his face squashed like leather against the glass of the back door, *aruf-ruf-ruf*. Neave's mother had told them that Dad had gone to live somewhere else because they'd argued a lot, but Neave hadn't once heard them quarrel.

Still watching, Neave can see her mother using the insides of her elbows to rub the sweat from her sunburnt brow and around her eyes. She's trying not to get too much earth all over her but it's powdered her face like a bad blusher. Neave thinks that perhaps it would be best if her mother made paper flowers, too. Looking at the Nostalgia in her hand, she notices how it's already turning green around the edges of its petals; her brother's right, she much prefers the flowers they've made.

The window creaks as Neave pushes it open again. Her mother looks up and waves but she isn't smiling. Neave stretches out her hand, holding what she had thought was Nostalgia in the air and as her mother smiles back, she lets go of it, waiting for the greening head to pirouette in the sky. Then she watches how it does anything but twirl and instead chooses to sink headfirst before pressing itself against the concrete below. By tomorrow, it will be trampled on, if not by a human foot, then by the sharp toes of birds or by heavy raindrops.

Her mother's back is as curled up as a bud now, one knee up as she completes the dustings around the tree; its partially-bloomed cherry blossoms are positioned in a way that look like a swirl of hair drooping down the back of her neck. Neave glances from the clique of flowers she'd stolen from, and towards the fallen Nasturtium. From there, she looks along the borders, where her mother has planted a row of all different flowers in a neat line, with perfectly-sized gaps between them. The man on the gardening programme had said Nasturtiums were all season long; he'd say the same about her mother.

Neave thinks about what her mother has told her before, how they should never expect perfect things, and she wonders if her Dad had ever listened. The weather doesn't feel so solid, now, she can feel a slight breeze burning her eyes and her cheeks, but she wants to keep them open. Dad must have listened because he took the caravan, and that wasn't perfect at all.

The garden wall appears entirely yellow from where Neave stands; every Nostalgia looks the same. Hearing the *chh chh chh* of her brother cutting more paper behind her, she can tell that his hands are still shaking. She's thinking of how she'll collect the Nostalgia and press it into a book heavy enough to flatten it into a photograph.

She attempts to shut the window again and as she does, it swings towards her forehead, causing her to stumble back onto one foot. The *chh* comes to an abrupt halt as it's replaced by David's laughter and as Neave topples towards him, she sees how happy his puffy eyes are, the tears streaming so quickly from them that he can't wipe the wetness away in time. His laugh roars until the desk shakes and he has to hold his stomach in place as it rolls up and down. Neave stands there, smiling at her brother, her big round eyes amazed by the impossibility of the picture.

My Sister, the Conductor

Samantha is deaf but she conducts music in her sleep. She moved in with me after our mother died. Now, only a plasterboard wall of Etruscan red separates our bedrooms, which means we're dangerously closer than before. The other side of her headboard is where my organ sits, its back pressed up and pumping against the decor, proud upon all thirteen haunches.

Samantha's used to getting what she wants. Back home, she only had to manipulate those puny hands in front of our faces and Mum would be rushing to her side. I'd hear the creak of the organ stool opening and Mum would be handing me a crinkled music book, smoothing down the centre of the pages with the backs of her knuckles and telling me to practise some new and complicated piece while she 'saw' to my sister yet again.

These days, I leap onto the leather cushion without being asked, always eager to experiment with some cacophony of chords for as long as I'm mentally able to. It began years ago, when I'd play for hours on end, only stopping when my back began to ache or my toes were raw with blisters. Only then, would I yank my headphones from the socket and like the blisters, prepare to burst with brilliance.

Thanks to my sister, however, it rarely happened that way. Instead, I'd turn around to find that there my audience was, fast asleep on the sofa, Samantha swaddled in Mum's arms and sucking her prawn of a thumb as though she was still a baby. Mum always reminded me that my sister was younger than me by seven years and unfortunately, always would be. She said it whenever my mouth was open and ready to object to something: probably the fact I was being served food *after* Samantha, which was most likely some sickening pasta meal of *Samantha's* choice, or maybe it was that I was once again being told I had to style Samantha's hair every morning because she wanted it to be exactly the same as mine. Always well behaved, unlike my sister, I keep my mouth shut.

One time, when I'd put on my headphones but hadn't begun to play, I heard Mum whispering, 'We're like two peas in a pod,' as they laid cheek-to-cheek beneath a blanket. Samantha's eyes were closed, unlike mine, and it made me mad that Mum's love was wasted on her. That night, I packed my book away and tucked myself into bed with as many layers as possible, slotting the duvet tightly underneath me on either side. I decided that when we next ate, I'd push peas into every pasta tube on Samantha's plate and watch her retch on them. As soon as I was old enough, I gladly moved out of the house to give them the space they always wanted.

The organ was the first item I took with me. It was the only thing I felt truly belonged to me since Samantha had been alive. Ever since she moved in, I could play it whenever I liked and she didn't realise. You see, she doesn't know how loud she can be during the night; neither does she know how often I creep into her room after being woken up by her dull groans. Then I watch her sleeping. I hate that she can sleep. It's become a habit of mine to sit upon the ottoman at the foot of her bed until the buttons have left round dents on the backs of my thighs as I try to place a rhythm or tempo with the continual swing of her arms.

It often looks as though Samantha's painting a wall, the way her hand brushes up and down. I sometimes wonder what colour she'd prefer, since I painted all these rooms red, never expecting anyone to stay. She'd probably choose a sickening yellow like the colour of her hair, but she never paints for long enough because a sharp wave led by her index finger always strikes through it all and just as my eyes – so tired from watching – adjust to a new pattern, it all comes to an abrupt end and there she is, snoring again, a percussive lion wrapped in cotton. Sometimes, I tuck her in more tightly.

It's only when she's entirely still that I come back to my room to play. Sometimes I just drape my hands over the keys like fallen pentagrams and see what they do, spreading out the messy sounds like an orchestra tuning up. I feel a release as it pours from my fingertips like blunt explosions, then once I have the mess out of my system, I play properly. It begins with nineties pop songs, power ballads and folk songs like 'Scarborough Fair' over and over again, and after that, I improvise, hoping for something on its way to revolutionary – you see, I'm the one who knows music here, I teach it, not Samantha. I focus on my framed Grade 8 certificates trembling upon the wall in front of me; you don't achieve those for nothing, and I imagine Samantha's brain being nudged along, or her puffy face vibrating with the ring of funeral music.

Samantha's never irked by anything, trust me, I've tried. That's where we differ. Imagine how scared I was when I first heard the groans: a horrible, ghost-like murmur slithering into my dreams. I woke up frozen to the spot, determined my bed sheets were strangling me and that there was someone else in my home. Then I remembered there was, of course, and that dull groan was my sister's strange version of speech, so I ran into her room, the one I'd generously loaned to her. I was truly, truly concerned that she was hurt in some way.

When I fell through the doorway, I saw that she was perfectly fine, of course, Samantha always is. Her eyes were closed and her face was painted with that same, wicked smile she wore on the sofa with our mother years ago, it was just that her arms kept moving. I tried going back to sleep but the groans kept

109

interrupting; I'd dream about zoos where I was trapped in a cage with a snarling lion and I'd curl up in the corner, feeling its breath upon me as I shook myself to sleep. Now, I am the lion.

I began to lie in wait in Samantha's room: I hoped my staring would somehow prevent the shamble of sound flowing from her mouth, which I still couldn't understand, sounds I could only claw onto for a second as her tongue was reeled in and out. The only thing it left me with was a selfish collection of flat notes. As dawn would break through the window, I couldn't help but notice the mess she'd made of the room, her clothes flung over the furniture, every surface covered with some sort of useless clutter. I know this house is only rented but it's still mine, yet there she was, conducting over the top of it all; the disrespectful Samantha.

I decided it was impossible that she was singing – because her arms, they fly in and out to form these giant double-u shapes, then as though she's opening and closing curtains, or kneading some large belly of dough with both hands, then slapping it onto a surface and tapping it with some magic wand. She'd never even heard music but her dramatic arm gestures and those theatrical, self-indulgent expressions of hers suggested the use of a baton. No, I felt sure, watching her disgusting mouth, that she was definitely trying to speak.

Sometimes, her eyes would open, just for a brief moment, but they didn't look at me, they only saw the shadows of us both on the ceiling. We were never very good at communicating. Years ago, when Mum wasn't close by, I often misinterpreted what Samantha was saying and we inevitably ended up fighting. She had no limits, the way she flung those arms and legs at me all at once, silent but deadly.

Thankfully, since she was half my size, I was able to brave the hits then lock my whole body around her as she scratched at me, until she had no space to move her limbs anymore. I used to feel her struggling for a few seconds, then hear her snivelling turn into a slow weep as she gave up. It was all down to her frustration after all; she was the one who couldn't be bothered to speak to me. Then she'd run to our Mum with her face still soggy and her hands flying again. Mum would tell me to go to my room and to stay there until she told me any different. I wasn't even allowed to play the organ. One time, I tiptoed downstairs in the middle of the night. It turned out; she'd forgotten she was supposed to say anything at all. There she was, sleeping alone on the sofa, her poor arms hanging over the end, worn out by Samantha's neediness, since Mum was the only person she could fluently speak to.

Every night that I sat on the ottoman, watching Samantha's arms dance and her voice jabber on, it was natural that I boiled up inside. If she was talking to Mum, I wanted to hear what they had to say, but there I was again, the daughter watching their hands fly past one another like a swarm of stiff butterflies, one and then the next, leaving nothing behind them but empty air I couldn't understand, the hands sometimes clasping together like halves, and as usual, leaving no space for a third. After a while, my chin would drop towards my chest for brief moments of doziness but I still only found myself in the scenes of a decade ago; my mother helping with Samantha's homework at the kitchen table whilst I sat alongside, trying to chew porridge as loudly as I could but finding it impossible to be told off. Our mother had become so adept at signing that she sometimes forgot to say anything out loud, and soon, the butterfly-hands had grown into birds, so I felt trapped at the edge of some circular storm as it rolled around in front of me, with no break for me to step inside it.

This time, I suppose I couldn't stand it anymore, so the next night, I decided I'd record my sister's gestures one by one. I'd never been bad at sketching, so I began to illustrate her on every blank page: in some, her arms were mid-snapping together in the

111

same way a child pretends to be a crocodile, and in the others, she'd already snapped. After several sketches, I realised that many of them portrayed what would appear to an onlooker to be someone possessed: she was so animalistic and out of control, the way her arms knotted together above her bed as she tossed and turned. Flicking through the pages from beginning to end made it look like an exorcism and I suppose the guilt crept up on me a little but it was only because I'd had enough. I still couldn't work out what any of it meant.

That's when I began to retreat to my room. I stuffed my ears with cotton wool, turned the organ's volume up to maximum and played as loudly as I could until the large speaker buzzed in front of my knees, the wall shook behind it and the pedals smashed into the floor. I wanted my sister to wake up, I wanted to interrupt the conversation between her and our mother. I thought about Samantha's head thumping, being banged against the solid, oak headboard and I didn't care. I was even angrier when I realised none of it made any difference. Every time this happened, we'd just wake up the next morning and welcome each other with the same shadows, stretching like semibreves under our eyes.

* * *

Last night, I stayed up late again. I couldn't quite give up on Samantha, you see, so I picked up the notebook and examined its contents; a conglomeration of my sister's miserable face. The black graphite was grey since I'd slammed the book shut so many times but it actually looked better that way. Parts of her had smudged like echoes onto the next pages, which left pieces of her face missing. She looked frightening. I'd have to accurately translate what remained, so remembering there was a whole shelf of books my sister had brought with her when she moved in a few months ago, I crept into her room and found an old pocket book called *The Basic Book of Sign Language*. It seemed strange that I'd never been introduced to this book before, its glossy pages led me through an array of Sign basics: the numbers, the alphabet, greetings, and locations. It was simple, but none of them matched up to my drawings.

I picked up a more complex book, since my sister had never been especially simple either, then I sat at the kitchen table to pore through it. I began to compare its diagrams with my drawings, its words with sounds, but it was entirely tedious; most were incomparable and the rest were unrecognisable. All I could identify were meaningless filler words like 'Oh,' or 'Uh,' which I could have worked out for myself since hearing them so many times through the red wall. Samantha's inconsiderate like that.

* * *

'What — *are* — you — doing?'

There was a voice interrupting a strange dream, where my face was being pushed up against a wall. One minute it was my voice, then it was Samantha's, definitely Samantha's, but somehow in my head. Everything echoed while I was up against the wall.

Once I was fully awake, the voice had returned to its usual sound, full of too much tongue and chin, with not enough space to articulate. I'd fallen asleep at the kitchen table, so my nose was flat against the oak and Samantha was alongside me, her arms moving faster than any conductor could conduct, even for an exceptional orchestra. Her enthusiasm was like a spritely phone call too early in the morning but according to the clock, it was one in the afternoon.

'What — are — these?'

My cluttered kitchen was shifting back into view. Samantha was holding my notebook below her chin and flicking through it page after page, threatening herself with a paper cut. She was

113

looking at every smudged drawing; each one a contorted hand, arm and face. 'Is — this — me?' she asked. The most solid leftovers of the sketches were her big, round eyes, which I'd stabbed in extra hard with the pencil. The real Samantha was conducting again, her hands flapping like a hen trying to fly.

'Yes, it's you,' I said, looking directly at her, 'Of *course* it's you. Who else would it be? There's no one else around here who talks like you, in your own, special language. Not anymore!' I noticed the mugs hanging on the wrong hooks behind her, as well as the juice standing ignorantly outside the fridge, and it made me mad.

Samantha's teeth were clenched together; her tongue threatening between them, then managing to get caught in its own bite. My tongue unguardedly did the same as she struggled. She'd even left the salt and pepper entirely the wrong way around on the table, their backs turned against one another.

I spoke instead of her. 'So, yes, I *did* watch you sleeping, I saw you talking to Mum and I've been writing it all down!' I was irritated by the slow sensibility to my voice. I looked at my notebook in her shaking hands. It was wide open but there was something odd about the images, something embellishing them; they looked like dark flecks of blood, as though the illustration of her was coughing them up.

Slowly, my sister began her irritating habit of conducting again, more carefully this time, her arms wide and her shoulders shrugging. 'What — do — you — mean? I — miss — Mum — have — you — seen — her?' she asked. Usually, when she spoke, she showed a range of expressions but this time, her face was deadpan and her eyes tormented. I didn't know why she bothered to use her hands when I couldn't understand any of it. If anything, it made me miss my mother. Samantha has always been thoughtless.

'You know very well that I haven't seen her,' I said.

'Oh,' she said, using no hands at all.

114

'But *you* have.'

The innocent face I'd been looking at for seventeen years was still confused.

'You talk to Mum in your sleep,' I added, 'that's why I sketched it all. I wanted to know what you were both saying!'

My sister picked up the book again and began to flick through the pages more frantically. Her hands were trembling as though they were suffering with spasms and she wasn't even giving me that fierce look of hers, which I was sure she could still do. I kind of wished she would but instead she just mumbled to herself in a way I couldn't decipher, and instead of throwing the book across the room, gently handed it back to me.

'Your — drawings — they're — very — good,' she said. Since speech is difficult for Samantha, her words are always chosen carefully. 'No — conversations — with — Mum,' she added, smiling with one side of her mouth, her head shaking back and forth. 'Always — nightmares — since — she — died,' she said. My stomach lurched. Samantha looked terrified again. 'I — didn't — know — my — hands — moved — in — the — night — they — do — ache.' She was clasping them tightly together as though punishing her fingers with a tight grip for all the trouble they'd caused, and shaking her head so fast that I just wanted to lock my body around hers as I did years ago, until she became still.

I took Samantha's hands and held them for a while to stop their shuddering, the long, spindled fingers folding over as she clenched her fists inside mine. Hers were just like Mum's; the same, predominant knuckles. Why did their hands even have to be the same? When Mum used to play the organ with me, her fingers just sprawled across the keyboards, scuttling up the octaves like spiders. The spiders must have died when my sister came along, leaving my stumpy hands to continue alone.

As Samantha's hands unfolded, I noticed the red caught beneath her nails.

115

'What's that?' I asked.

'Nightmares,' she said, her face worried as she held one hand in her other and began to walk away. One of her arms was ushering me out of the kitchen and towards her bedroom. When we were in there, standing at the foot of her bed, she pointed to a place just above the headboard. There were long scratches down the paintwork, only white flecks like the wings of flies underneath.

'I — thought — I — could — feel — the — walls — moving — around — me.'

She looked so frightened. I pictured her scraping at the red. It would've taken a long time to get through those layers to the other side; five coats it had taken for the dark colour I'd originally wanted, though it had never quite felt dark enough. Her claw marks were further down, too, a long, jagged trail down the left and right. 'Sorry — about — the — paint,' she said.

'It doesn't matter,' I told her, only thinking about all the nights I'd played so loudly, wanted her head to shake with frustration.

I led her into my room where the organ was, then set Samantha to stand alongside with her back against the wall, two hands pressed flat against it, then I sat down in my familiar position upon the organ stool. I stuffed cotton wool into my ears, pressed the organ's 'on' switch and slid my right foot onto the expression pedal, ready to begin. When I played, I at first saw no change in my sister's face, but as I tilted my right foot forward on the pedal as though it was an accelerator, the organ became louder and her bare feet seemed to press harder into the carpet pile. I played and played and played until the speaker and the wall behind her buzzed. My sister, suddenly feeling the pulse of the organ in both her hands and feet, had her eyes wide open.

I took Samantha's hand again and placed her palm down upon the wooden surface of the organ itself and she smiled as the vibration shot through her; the electric jolt of music that I'd never

116

imagined we'd enjoy together. Suddenly, her other arm lifted and there she was, conducting again, with a more directed swoop than the one I'd seen so many times while she'd been sleeping.

'Not — a — nightmare — at — all,' Samantha tried to shout, entranced by my hands as they met in the middle of the upper and lower keyboards, then parted again, working hard to orchestrate the experience.

On the notebook left open on the top of the organ, I saw the illustrations of Samantha turned into something dark and I slammed the book shut. I imagined the images transforming all on their own, becoming more curved and less jagged. Their mouths were opening and closing but smiling. I continued to play but kept looking at her, suddenly realising how she'd coped since Mum, her only listener, had died. Her hands must have found it difficult to rest and so, just like me, she'd kept using them, I just hadn't known why.

When the music ended, the tears bubbled up in her eyes and fell as little shocks as she fell into my arms. *I — wish — I — could — speak — to — her* — she was saying, *I — miss — her.*

'I've missed her for seventeen years,' I said, but she didn't hear me, of course; there's a lot I say to her that she doesn't hear. I was surprised by how tight the embrace was. I don't know why I hadn't noticed before but we were almost the same height. Her hands were pressed flat upon my shoulder blades but with the same strength as my own around her rib cage, which I could feel like broken staves through her back. Her diaphragm was already reverberating, the volts of her heartbeat powering inside as though it might burn through and fuse with mine. As usual, we were out of time with each other. It was Samantha's breath that slowed down and waited for mine. For the first occasion in years, we were entwined like a treble clef and the organ was silent.

'Anne—' Samantha said, gesturing two hands towards her chin, which I knew meant 'thank you.' Then she gave me a look

I'd witnessed before, one she'd given to my mother; one of entire trust, as though her world didn't really belong to her at all – and now, she was looking at me the same way, as though it belonged to me; an object I'd *never* intended to bring from home.

I've since peeled back the carpet, so Samantha's feet will feel the vibrations even more through the wooden floor. I intend to hold her hand upon the speaker, so she can feel the beat pierce through every one of those skinny fingers. She can lay her cheek flat across the top of the organ and I'll mouth the words to the rhythm. I'll show her again and again and again, and if she doesn't grasp it straightaway, we'll play as many times as it takes until we sound the very best we can. I'll ask her in Sign, 'how does it feel, Samantha?' and I'll wait for her response until it's nothing other than perfect, just like her. Isn't it my duty, after all, to look after the guest in my house?

The Bereaved

For a time, I resembled the coffee mug on the window-sill: mendable, but with cracks so sporadic, it was difficult to predict when I would next shatter. When it finally happened, it was with all the silence of the first time. My wife witnessed the blood-encrusted vomit on my face and screamed. If I was the mug, she would have picked me up and thrown me once more, my cracked pattern jigsawing at the prospect. Then she would have taken the glue from her pocket and pieced me back together again.

These days, she is awake during the lifeless time of night, when the air is thick with sleeping people. She tries to close her eyes against the dark but the lengthy echo of silence is what causes her body to sweat, rotates it in eternal frustration, then strands her in the centre of this dire, domestic island.

There were visitors once. Flowers were left on the doorstep as a show of respect. Our home, just one of a terrace, is marked by the crisped cadavers of carnations in the porch. They have broken away into bleats of deep red upon the concrete tiles. Cakes have been left to turn stale in their boxes.

The mood inside is similar to that of a bleak bed and breakfast. There are too many dull guests gorging on grief. They are dark, lanky beings, drifting like crane flies up the walls, then falling again, their ribs racked under bare-skinned backs and the heads of tenterhook necks attempting to climb and fall, climb and fall. There is a distant look in each eye as their heads lurch to the side. Wherever grief is, they reside, occupying the empty space until

119

the house is heaving with sorrow. Daylight whispers at the windows, but it is a stranger to us all.

One resident, after slumping to the floor, takes a moment to reorient, becoming a limp obstruction in the hallway. I tiptoe over his upturned body and cross the threshold, breaking into what feels like a bell jar of time. The smell of moth-balls tries to cling with dust to my nostrils. Something is sedate, everything, as my feet disrupt nothing but the leanings of the carpet pile. The rest of the residents are still climbing, picking at cobwebs, then dropping them like lace onto my shoulders. I try to remove them, but they are entwined in a way that brandishes me in a grey veil.

In the living room, I meet two armchairs sunken at the shoulders from the weight of dog-eared boxes of my belongings. They aren't packed to go anywhere. Instead, there are shirts with the shoulders still shaping them, draped all over the furniture like broken people and as I look around, I see that some of the residents are wearing my shoes.

Everything here once looked after, has been simultaneously abandoned. The dust-tongued rug is hunched up and unwagging, but lies beneath a mossy fish tank, the corpse of one fish trailing from the mouth of the other. I move towards the kitchen, following the rest of the wilted petals but as I step onto the tiled floor, the phone rings and a man's voice interrupts. I look to the hallway but the words don't follow my ears.

'I'm afraid we're not here at the moment…' says the voice, in a pitch I recognise. 'If you would like to leave a message…' Then it stutters a little. How could I have forgotten it so soon? A resident sitting at the kitchen table turns sharply towards me, then continues to nudge crumbs around the surface. The voice ceases to speak.

This room is in an equally slovenly state and stores little sustenance. The rings of the unclean oven hob are engraved and the sink is mounted with moulded plates, flies glued to solidified food. Mice are eating what could have been the ingredients of something substantial and the kettle stands wrapped up in its own wire. I remember its distinctive whine, its fast whistle over that voice. Then there is a bleep, slow like that of someone flatlining.

The voice has instead transformed to a lady's voice, crackling between careful pauses.

'Dear, I'm worried about you,' it says, 'I know it's been very difficult but...' Then I hear something different, a drone above me. The resident at the table is wrestling the bread crumbs with her fingertips, trying to push them together like Play-Doh. The hum turns into a wail. There is the slow applause of a clock on the wall as I leave the room to ascend the stairs and visit my wife.

The landing seems further away than before as I climb its back, each step a hurdle of socks and underwear as I impose on raw memory. I look behind me to the resident in the hallway: his grey body is twitching as he tries to sit up, but his eyelids are flickering as though they are still asleep through a dreadful dream. The arms of two others appear in a tug around my waist as I try to climb faster, but they eventually let go and I see a familiar belt slouched across the top step.

I hear the muffled wail through a door ajar enough for me to slip through, which uncurls to a loud howl as I enter the misery of magnolia. There is the bereaved, crouched helplessly upon an unravelling patchwork of my life, amongst a mound of my clothes, my dressing gown draped around her clothes-hanger shoulders. Her face is crumpled with pain but clearly tired from its perpetual foldings.

Even though she howls, the air remains still, a congregation of emptiness. I move closer to disrupt it, but as usual, my figure feels no gravity. As I join my wife at knee level, she wrenches the rope of my dressing gown tighter around her middle, the towelling spitting dust and my old aroma in my face. In the muskiness, paper begins to stick to my knees and as I begin to use my voice,

121

I at first think she is stopping me with one hand until the other reaches out, both of them in a hollow embrace. I begin to wonder if she can feel my presence but looking at her face so pale and bloodless, I can't even decipher whether her mouth is open or closed until I hear her sobs again. There are photographs of us mislaid around the room. I peel one away from my knee and smile just like I used to when I felt her hand in the same place.

Then the sobs stop. My wife is searching for something. I begin to doubt she will find it amongst the medley as her hands trace each item, searching for a particular piece. I feel the urge to touch the underneath of her wrist where it tickles, but she is crying so much that it quivers out of my reach, continuing to search the carpet, just as she had when frantically picking up the pills as though they were the beads of a broken necklace. It finally stops upon my knee, lingers. I remember now: home in the shape of this woman's hand.

But it moves again. She has found what she was looking for; a piece of paper folded up so small that it barely exists, like the pills, so small but altogether, deadly. She holds it as though it might leave. There weren't enough pills left to make a necklace. This place is hardly recognisable, with so many gathered fragments of me: odd gloves, a hat I rarely wore, old cigarettes and aftershave are dotted around the cluttered floor and soaking up every cavity. The wardrobe doors are open and my clothes have slipped in a landslide onto the carpet; shirts we used to argue over the ironing of are bent at the elbows in a heap of my old identities and trousers lie like the murder marks of dead men around the room. The blinds are shut and the curtains are drawn, hair-clipped together so the light in the room remains dim. I can just about see the mundane mosaic of my coffee mug scattered over the window-sill. My calendar still hangs on the wall, left open at January. It's now July.

The resident from the kitchen has followed me up and is sliding photographs of my face around with her stockinged toes. Around

122

her smooth heels are my old magazines and newspapers piled high. The residents are taking hold.

As my wife hoists her body up, I see that a mousy down has been allowed to creep over her calves. It's cold and erect, a bark of miserable pencil shavings. Oblivious to my visit, she stretches her arms above her head, fingers cobwebbed together. The dressing gown's tie loosens again, shedding from her body and falling to her bony ankles.

Released with a hoarded musk is the body of my young wife, age climbing the walls around her like stubborn fungi. She's beautiful, but I don't attempt to touch her narrowing outline as it gazes through me to the sight of something else – her hair grasping the hollow bulb of her face – then drops straight to the floor with a whimper. For a moment, she'd forgotten.

Above the navy of my dressing gown is a crouched body, her greased hair its only covering. She embraces the gown with a fierce look in her eyes and as always, it yields to her weakness, her body sinking as one does at a graveside, tail-bone dipping into the dust. Her shoulders are so hunched together from whimpering that the blades of her back look like they might never straighten again, her body has control over nothing but the piece of paper in her right fist. As she opens it, I see her lips miming:

Sorry and *forgive me* and *thank you* and *I wish* and *love* and *death* and *escape* and *pain* and *trapped* and *sorry* and *forgive me* and *I wish…*

I feel myself crumbling as each word seems to twist something in my stomach, beginning like the sting of cramp but growing to a sickening pain that turns everything into more of a blur as she continues and I whisper alongside.

Love and *death* and *hurts* and *friends* and *family* and *love* and *pain* and

   alone,   *alone,*   *alone,*

                           forgive me.

I look at her again but her head is still bent. From her vacancy, I know the words she has read sound as empty as those engraved on a sympathy card, her neck stiff, eyes still.

'Forgive me,' I try to utter, but my lips only mime too. The bereaved looks towards my face with an expression I've seen once before: there had been vomit acryliced to my skin and a clique of pills around my feet. I was heaped in a corner, head against the bookcase and my knees beneath my chin. She'd retched at the sight of me. I remember my eyes seeing something differently. Then she touched me and screamed.

   She is screaming again…

   …and the air has begun to pulsate in sync with the sound. I feel as though I could topple, but my toes clench the carpet. Before I take another step, a swell of grey glissades past me. All the residents have followed me upstairs and are beginning to swarm around us, their legs clumsily crossing over each other and fighting for space. My wife is shaking as though she can feel their presence, but I've been visited by the residents before, when I was curled up in a ball, trying to unwrap myself from unexplainable sadness. Waking up every day at noon, the world appeared very slightly out of focus, I cradled a heavy burden, which sent my life rotting into the ether. Sometimes, it was interrupted by a flurry of cries. It was then that I began to see the grey figures. I tried to blink them away but they kept calling.

   Looking closely at the unearthly residents, I know the droll habits of each one. My wife's uninterested. Her face looks up, but straight through me to the calendar on the wall; days are blacked out like decayed teeth. The paper in her hands however, is an unperturbed white. She reads the words for a second time and I think back to my cries from this very room when there was still a single strobe of light to look at through the v-shape gap in the top of the curtains, until darkness returned so regularly, so unpredictably, and I only dreaded its visits.

The residents are definitely taking hold. They are doubling and tripling around us, closing in and rotating like a circle of ring a-rosies where both of us are in the centre, already down. They're pushing against us and tightening around us like a boa constrictor; we are face to face, my wife's breath moist upon my neck. She begins to whimper once more, yanking the dressing gown tighter around her as she does. As dawn creeps further into the room, I see through the curtains to the world I've stepped out of, too large for my wife to step out into without practise.

'I can't forget,' she says again, knowing that no one can hear, her head still and her eyes sinking together. My face feels as rotten as the day she found me, as vacant and detached. A spider creeps across it. My wife's eyes, with the slant of their brows are questioning *why?* But I don't respond. Why does anything ever happen? She seems to search my face and sickness tugs at my stomach. This house aches from the core for something to fill it. 'You actually did it,' she says, loudly and clearly. 'You actually…'

The residents have dissipated and are climbing the walls again, but my wife and I remain intimate, her head almost bowed upon my shoulder. If she could hear me, I'd explain how much I didn't *want* to do it. It felt like the only answer for so much pain. I'm crouching over her now as she curls up, begging for a different reality. My letter is once again lost amongst the quarry of me and eventually, her irises freeze, her body resists, any strength she had has dissolved into my lap. We're in the same place for perhaps the very first time.

'It's everything you can't see,' I finally whisper, thinking of the hectic house around her, as she twists and turns again like a doll in my bare hands. She cries into her knees, rocks back and forth, encasing her legs, then drops onto her side, wailing. 'Why?' she cries with her head in her hands and I know the pulling and yearning she feels in her stomach.

I look out the window and see the fickle Welsh weather; sun breaking through the clouds, then giving up. I sense the brush of another spider crossing my face but I still don't move it, allowing it to curtain my hair with its spun thread. The arms of my wife reach out but I stay back until she collapses again, rolling onto her spine with a helpless whimper. The residents are dropping from the walls and landing in piles upon the carpet before they stand, then start climbing all over again.

Breaking the whimper is a voice bellowing through the floorboards. It's the slow murmur of my answer-phone stuttering, followed by the sustained bleep and the same lady's voice speaking.

'Hello again, it's me, love,' but the sound of a little voice from the background breaks to the forefront, transforming into the cry of a child. *Life goes on,* people say.

Life   goes   on.

'He's asking for you,' is what I make of the lady's voice, loudening through the ceiling; my mother-in-law. 'He's wondering where you are,' she adds, but before I clutch onto any more words, the wailing begins again. My wife has shifted back into focus; a weak heap of bony woe. She drains the remains of an exhausted sob, as though she's realising how quickly time is passing even as she collects her breath. She tries to stand, but the resident from the kitchen presses her down at the shoulders. Three faces look up at me from a photo at my wife's weak ankles. For one of them, I hear our son's cries. *Ma-ma ma-ma,* then nothing.

My wife composes herself and at first only rocks like a roly-poly toy before launching her body through the resident's grey arms and finding a stance that doesn't topple. She stares directly at each resident around us, as though acquainting herself with each lost face. If they weren't so limp, she'd shake their hands, finally acknowledging the feeling.

She walks carefully out of the room, carrying nothing but my dull dressing gown. The dust spits at her feet but her breath is the only sound I hear. It's here that I notice the expression of the residents changing for the first time, the void in their eyes filled with longing. Nevertheless, my wife walks towards the bathroom and I follow her in, watch her beginning to shower, observe as she crouches upon the porcelain floor of the bath and feels the warm waterfall upon her grieving, goose-bumped skin.

I imagine I can feel it upon me too, our aches simultaneously disappearing, deep worn out muscles numbing under the boil. This is the longest time she hasn't cried for. Her eyes are closed and her frayed mouth is open. She buries her flat chest away from me, beneath wet arms crossed in front of her knees and she lies down at the base, water still beating upon her.

When she eventually steps out of the bathroom, she's dressed in her own clothes, much baggier than before. On the landing, the residents face her in a queue. My wife looks less surprised walking past them, almost lost among the line of grey faces. They've been waiting. They're adorned in my shirts and trousers, walking versions of the broken men in our bedroom. With free rein, they seem to walk in more of a stride and they no longer bother to climb the walls. They're standing in my shoes, toes pressed right to the tips of the leather, more comfortable than I ever made them feel.

Soon, she clears a path downstairs and begins to tidy the mess in the kitchen, closing cupboard doors and scraping food into the bin. Every now and then, she sits in the living room, upon the tired armchair with her head in her hands and she moans at the injustice. As I blink, I see the house emptying around us.

The residents follow my wife into every room, this time the kitchen. They're picking up saucepans and with no ingredients to use, placing every utensil back in the same place. She's making cups of tea and setting them around the house as though for each resident. She feels them dithering around her but she continues to tidy up, their presence as ignored as wallpaper. She's increasingly tolerant of these thieves as the days go on, each evening blackmailed grey and stumbling into the next.

Then she clears up the crumbs, places pots in the sink, dusts the shelves in the living room and undrapes the armchairs. This house is gradually resembling the place we forged together, argued and laughed in, where we brought a blend of us both home in a baby's shawl. *I'm so sorry.*

As grief subsides, the residents are itching to leave, starved of their surroundings, their bored bodies twitch like the one in the hallway. The clock has clapped so many times that its hands must ache and new dust is beginning to settle on the carpet.

I watch to see if my wife will glue my mug back together one more time, but she's only rearranged it upon the kitchen table. She sits for a while, staring at each piece and I wonder what she's waiting for. *Forgive me,* I say, *forgive me.* The doorbell has begun to ring, but she doesn't budge at the sound, her eyes are open, but ignorant. Then it rings again, a long drill of a bell, so constant that she has to stand up.

Eventually, I see her traipsing towards the door. She opens it to visitors; my mother-in-law, who carries a large container of food in one hand, with her grandson clutching onto the other. He releases his grip and gallops throughout the house, exploring every space, panting and gibbering as though silence was never here. My mother-in-law stands in the porch, smiling, then strides through and throws open the curtains of every downstairs window.

128

My wife's not ready for this, I think, feeling daylight harsh upon my face. Then I hear her voice from another room.

'You mustn't touch that,' but it's too late, having followed her back into the kitchen, I see that our son has headed straight for what must have appeared to be a colourful jigsaw. Before there is a chance to stop him, he picks up one of the pieces, then quickly drops it again, recoiling at the sharpness of its edges upon his tiny fingers. The shock, like being bitten, has filled his eyes with tears, his bottom lip protruding as though this is entirely unreasonable.

My wife immediately checks over the fleshy palm of our son, holding it firmly in hers, then rotating it as though it's as delicate as the china. *Everything's going to be okay*, she says to him, *everything's going to be okay.* Then I watch her stoop down to embrace him, his little head drooping onto her shoulder and furrowing at the brow. My wife becomes angry at the pieces. She points at them, saying how terrible they are to have done such a thing, but our son points too, causing my wife to laugh, and then him to giggle in her arms, his chunky body already struggling to break free, sure that she will follow him.

Without a thought, she sweeps up each broken piece of china and discards them outside, away from little hands, before joining our son in a game of chase. I wait a while, I watch as she feeds him, as she gazes at him indulging in every spoonful and pointing at the reflection from the shining silver as it dances around the room, fascinated as it flickers through the open window, like a firefly. He flaps his arms, convinced that he might also fly, amazed at his own potential, and colour rises into my wife's cheeks as she can't help but smile; the recent wrinkles by the sides of her eyes pulling more tightly together the longer she watches him. It is here that I take my leave and the grey army of grief follows me outside, in single file.

129

The Girl in the Painting

Time was chipping away faster than Lizzie's grandmother had ever conceived. There she was again, hunched over the sink and scouring the dishes with red hands. Just a little more time and any hint of a rose-pattern would fade into each circle of white forever. She stacked the plates on the draining board and watched the sweat run from each, pale hill. Her husband was settled, as always, at the head of the table, opening the biscuit tin with fingers too stout to make it a simple procedure, whilst Lizzie, who would be spending more time there during the summer holidays, was perched two seats away.

Lizzie looked dumpier recently, her plump body finding it easy to hide her cold feet underneath it, but her grandmother wouldn't mention anything. She was much too aware of how touchy girls could be at this age; remembering herself in puffy dresses, ready to ripple if anyone dared to brush past her. There was definitely something different, though; Lizzie seemed to be much too focused on the painting on the wall to notice her grandmother's face wrinkling up at her, and even though her grandfather's head was looming wherever she tried to look, she found a way to gaze straight through it. She had seen the painting on many occasions, it was impossible to avoid the wooden frame of almost an arm-span either way. It was of the farmhouse in which they lived: white and rectangular with only a faint, grey outline from rain and age, and an uncommonly curved black, slate roof. Lizzie had never noticed how it made her feel so many fields away as she counted the six, square windows scattered across the front,

131

revealing the glow of each room inside. Each one seemed to push her back further and further to exactly where the artist must have sat, right up on the hill, his easel astride in front of him as he threw earth at the canvas.

It was done by a man, she could tell from the ruthlessness of the bumps and scratches in the deep green, as though they'd been dug and refilled time and time again. She wondered why he would have painted it, why he'd been roaming the fields like that, not that roamers need reason. Her mother had never mentioned wanderings, probably because she wasn't the type to understand how someone could obtain the time, especially if it was to sit and paint. She was always too busy, continually moving, which Lizzie found strange when her mother was born in a farmhouse which was so still. She never stepped over its threshold for very long, either, as though some strange uneasiness kept her out.

Lizzie was so transfixed by those layers, which gave the painting the illusion of growing out of the wall, the whole house moving towards her. She wanted, so much, to run her finger along those bumps, curious to find the very last part to have been painted, the section closest to her. Lizzie assumed it was the house that was the nearest, and she scanned over it for a while before spotting anything unusual: left to right, then top to— then, there, in the right-hand corner amongst some foliage, was a bright red fleck of paint, a solid, fire engine red standing out among the pastel shades! With a closer look, there was no questioning its existence, so isolated but small enough to slyly disappear whenever it decided. Lizzie uncrossed her legs, placed her feet onto the icy kitchen floor and leaned over the table, her palms flat on the crumb-covered surface and her eyes squinting.

The little splash of red formed a more specific shape, triangular, but imperfect like the lines of their farmhouse, and above the red was a small oval of pink, which comprised two, tiny black dots. Altogether, the strokes of paint became a

132

trespasser, a girl in a red dress. Her face was so blurred that it looked unfinished, neglected not long before the end. She was peeping through the hedge, with her back bowing at the top beneath chestnut plaits, and in her left hand, was a basket almost half the size of her body. Lizzie, amazed, slid back down onto her chair.

'Nan. Is that you in the painting?'

Her grandmother's head turned, surprised but smiling all the same.

'Yes, chick, that's me. Why d'you ask?' Lizzie shrugged, and then thought of how strange it was that the girl stood so close to the edge of the picture. It was almost as though the artist had tried to amend some kind of mistake.

Whilst Lizzie looked up, biting hard on her bottom lip, her grandfather smiled, his wind-burnt cheeks even redder from the hot tea he was drinking.

'Who painted it?' Lizzie asked, as her grandfather, with a *haaaa* and a heavy hand, placed his empty mug on the table.

Her grandmother, a little startled, said, 'Well, the love of my life, actually. 'He lived over on the next farm.' And as her words melted into a sigh, Lizzie's grandfather cleared his throat so loudly that it drowned out the rest. Lizzie considered that he may not have been who her grandmother was referring to. It was strange that they may have once loved people other than each other. The girl in red's shoulder now sloped so low that the basket brushed against the grass.

'What's in the basket?' Lizzie asked. Her grandmother was drying her hands as though intending to rub away any softness. 'Just some fruit, chick. Nothing too important.'

Lizzie's head flopped towards the saucer of biscuits her grandfather had slid in front of her, but as it did, she swore the little girl in red tiptoed further onto the painting. Her original position would have been hidden by a wider frame, whereas now, she stood on the other side of the hedge and clearly within the field that surrounded the house. She was looking over both shoulders as though she was frightened of being followed.

'Right then,' Lizzie's grandfather placed his hands on both knees to push himself up, then stretched so his chest puffed out like a maroon-breasted robin. 'I'm off to feed those lambs before bed. I'll leave you girls to it.' He laid a hand upon his wife's shoulder, and then disappeared outside.

'Nan, I'm sure the girl in the painting is moving!'

'Now now, Lizzie, love. I'm sure you're just tired after the long drive.'

* * *

In her bedroom, faraway from all the other rooms and right above the icy pantry, Lizzie curled up, hoping to escape her imagination. Her mother had always said it could inflict the strangest of things. Even before the light was off, this room had a life of its own; her mother's childhood seemed to creep across the wallpaper, and the carpet, mixed-brown like Alsation fur.

'What've you seen?' Lizzie whispered to the bear on the bedside table, afraid to hug him. She wondered if the room minded her nestling in.

The floorboards sighed as her grandfather whistled along the landing. Lizzie switched off the lamp. With no lights from houses nearby, she listened to the stillness for a while, the only other sound the clock ticking, its second hand chopping like wood. Even the birds had gone to sleep.

As she waited for the flannelette sheets to absorb her, Lizzie counted sheep racing each other over fences, but the blur of black and white only roused their farmhouse into mind. The girl in red reappeared as though she'd been standing there the entire time, watching, then weaving through the kissing gate and tiptoeing

134

red dots across Lizzie's eyelids. Eventually, Lizzie landed in a dream where she was the one walking field after field, lost amongst the green and unable to find her way home, until she eventually saw a glimpse of the familiar white shape of the familiar farmhouse in the distance.

When she awoke, much earlier than usual thanks to the cockerel, she tiptoed to the window to witness him, perched proudly upon the closest barn to the house. With her bare feet sinking into the carpet, Lizzie thought of all the animals stirring, those lambs springing up out of milky dreams, and she knew she didn't want to miss a moment of it.

Her grandmother was preparing lunch in the kitchen, and there, as expected, the girl in the painting had moved again, this time, even closer to the farmhouse. Lizzie rubbed her eyes so the sky in the painting looked less stormy, but the girl was still standing there, looking up at the house as though it was some sort of predator, its door ready to open up and its tongue, like a cow's, ready to roll out and snatch her inside. Lizzie blinked again and as she did, the girl's basket fell to the grass, her mouth agape as though she'd dropped a lot more than a 'nothing of importance'. She bent over it for a while, her arm stretching to pick it up.

'Lizzie,' her grandmother shouted, not seeing her in the doorway, 'fetch your breakfast. It's on the aga.' The food was good at drawing Lizzie in. There was something about breakfast that made her feel more at home.

'Thanks. Where's Granddad?'

'Oh, he's just down the yard seeing to the cows. He'll be back later.'

Beef was cooking, Lizzie could smell it, so rich that she could picture it layered upon their Sunday Dinner plates; the foundation, a gravy-filled Yorkshire pudding. She remembered watching her grandfather shout at the cows, slapping them with

135

sticks as though they were coach horses, patting their sides with his large, flat hand, or just as likely, luring them in with a loud shout, *sooksooksooksook sooksooksooksook,* beating the side of the metal shed until they were taken in by the tinny echo as though he was some musical master. Lizzie looked down at her breakfast, a modest plate of browned bacon and the smallest of sausages that she'd already almost finished, everything so crisp that it crackled on the fork, then crumbled into tasty flavours in her mouth.

'Don't forget, there's extra bread on the table if you want it,' her grandmother added.

Just a few feet above the slices, the painting loomed.

'Nan! The girl in the painting has definitely moved!'

Her grandmother flinched as the knife she'd been using sliced into the end of her finger.

'Nan, are you okay?'

'Oh, don't fuss, Lizzie. Look, all sorted!' She seemed angry, already binding the miserable finger with a handkerchief from her pocket. It was dotted with blood.

'Shall I go and help Granddad, then?' Lizzie took her last mouthful, worried that she'd rushed and would therefore begin the day in the same way her mother tended to.

'No, he's okay for now, chick. Perhaps you could help me with the food instead.'

'Okay. Maybe I could go for a walk later!'

'Well, you'd best wait until after lunch, but you mustn't wander too far!'

Her grandmother turned back to the chopping board. The sounds seemed to echo as though she was miles away, trying to guillotine the thick air between them. Even though her finger was bandaged, the red was still trailing out.

Her thoughts had returned to the past. This was a woman who had been wormed into at thirteen, her innocence broken and the damage disguised as puppy fat under puffy dresses. Months later, whimpering and panting in a field, she was unable to run from the wriggling baby.

The strange man clutched her bony wrist so tightly that she panicked her fingers might turn blue. 'You'd better take care of that,' he'd said, looking so deeply into her eyes as she lay beneath the rose bush, and so afraid of greenflies crawling up her bare legs, that she had done nothing but listen. The dollish thing had looked up at her, its face for the first time a weight in her arms instead of her womb, but just another stranger to her. Then two greenflies landed on its chest. She remembered that part well; they were fluttering side-by-side like a four-leaf clover, causing the baby to cry even louder. Her own cries sank back to her stomach. She knew that at home, at the farmhouse, things would be different now: their hearts knocked against each other from different directions.

* * *

Lizzie's day had been filled with food. Until now, she had presumed it was a family tradition to feed, feed, feed, but looking around her, and considering her own parents, she was the only one to, as a result, be so stocky. Not that she minded. She felt it brought weight to her feet as she walked around, a sort of commanding maturity, perhaps even something maternal in the way she had no choice but to embrace everything she held.

'See you later Nan,' Lizzie shouted, stealing one of the many cardigans from the coat hooks.

'Oh, hang on, Liz, it's up to you, but wouldn't you like to pick some flowers with me first?'

Unable to ignore the smell of lavender emanating from the wool around her shoulders, Lizzie smiled, she could get used to this. She'd warmed to life at the farmhouse, it was different somehow, even time felt different. The outdoors felt comforting, especially the idea of beauty being grown at home, then worn in a glass vase, there was something stable about it and Lizzie was already dreading her mother picking her up. She noticed the tremble in her grandmother's fingers as she picked each stem and placed it carefully into the basket. Her grandmother's face was so similar to her mother's, the same 'v' of wrinkles in the centre of the forehead. If someone were to say they looked like sisters, it would be believable.

'Nan, you must have been young having my mother.'

'Yes, too young,' she said, without looking at Lizzie, 'your mother was teased at school because of it, you know. I don't blame her for choosing a university so far away.'

'But why didn't she come back?'

'Well, you know, your mother's very career-focused. And I'm glad she made the most of her mind. God knows I didn't! And, well, she eventually met your father, and then had you later in life, when she knew she was ready, you know. Your mother's good like that.'

'So you weren't ready when you had Mum?'

'You like asking questions, don't you? Let's get these in a vase!' Lizzie couldn't help but feel that the air had become solid again. Within seconds, they were marching back to the house.

Lizzie's grandmother had a talent for giving nothing away. She felt like her mother had it too, though it seemed more present here, where the trees swayed, then suddenly became still.

As they entered the kitchen, Lizzie's grandmother collected a vase and filled it up at the sink, leaving Lizzie to once again stare at the painting. There was the girl in red, large and out of scale when compared with the landscape, as though she had just this second leapt back into the frame and not yet decided where to blend in. Then she was back in her previous position where she had dropped the basket, and her face looked a patchy white, blotted with so many tears that Lizzie feared her eyes might smudge themselves away.

'Nan, Nan you've got to look, the girl in the painting is upset!' This time, the girl looked directly at Lizzie, her hands locked together in prayer as she continued to cry.

'Nan!'

Her grandmother's eyes were reddening around the rims. She placed the vase gently alongside the sink. 'Liz, come and sit on the sofa with me,' she whispered. The tremble had taken to her voice. She took Lizzie's hand and pressed her own palm on top as though there was a secret hidden inside.

As soon as they sat down, she began, 'I know I told you the girl in the painting is me, love, and that's the truth, but the basket doesn't really hold fruit. No fruit at all.'

'What's in the basket? What's in it, Nan?'

Her grandmother spoke quickly, as though she was afraid that if she didn't explain all at once, she never would.

'It held a baby,' she mumbled, her chin lowering, 'your mother.' Lizzie couldn't imagine her mother ever being contained in something so small. The past was cracking open like wicker.

'I was only thirteen, Liz, the same age as you are now. But it wasn't from choice, I was forced by—' Lizzie's mouth hung open. Her grandmother let out a high-pitched sob, 'by a horrible—' Lizzie was already picturing some sort of beast. 'Man,' her grandmother added, her two red hands fluttering towards her face. Lizzie couldn't help but imagine her own stomach, a tiny body growing inside it. It was frightening. This wasn't the kind of story grandmothers were supposed to tell. The face of the girl in the painting suddenly became bloodless.

Lizzie's grandmother clenched her hand in front of her chest and jolted back against the sofa, trying to hold onto every next breath. Through the sobbing, she still managed to speak. 'I'll never forget those words, "you'd better—"' she gasped, '"'take care of that." My little baby was crying.' She tried to take another breath but the air wasn't there.

'Granddad! Granddad! Something's wrong with Nan,' Lizzie called. She could hear him kicking his wellies off at the back door.

'What, love? What's the matter?' he shouted, over the sound of the barking sheepdogs.

'Quickly, it's Nan!' As he passed through the kitchen, the oil painting fell face-down on to the table. 'You'd better take care of that, Liz,' he said, his thumb gesturing behind him, 'I'll see to your Nan.'

Lizzie couldn't move. Had those words really rolled out of her grandfather's mouth? She worried about the girl in the red dress who was probably crawling underneath the painting, her face squashed unwillingly against the table, and its deceitful biscuits – *unwillingly*. She stared at her grandfather, who looked fierce with concern for his wife, whose face was contorting, her eyes two explosions of wrinkles. He dropped a hand very gently upon her cheek but she only looked frightened, her feet fidgeting upon the carpet.

'I'd better call an ambulance,' he said, and Lizzie shuddered as the wool of his jumper brushed against her arm.

When the sirens arrived, electric blue flickered like lightning against the windows of the farmhouse. The Paramedics seemed to burst in and within minutes, they were sliding Lizzie's grandmother into the back of the ambulance as though it was a hearse and she was the coffin.

Lizzie's grandfather's hand grasped her shoulder as they climbed into the cramped space in the back of the ambulance. She could hear his exaggerated sniffle as he drew a handkerchief from his pocket, but his tears disgusted her, the way they contracted in his eyes. She tried not to look at him and instead thought of the farmhouse, shrinking in the distance.

* * *

Lizzie assumed there was something about hospitals that brought families closer together. Maybe it was the presence of so much blood that did it, made everyone magnetise towards those they knew. She was drawn toward her mother who was waiting at the entrance while her grandmother was quickly wheeled away. At that moment, Lizzie felt the most attached to her she ever had. Her grandfather, however, who was he all of a sudden? As they gathered around the grandmother's hospital bed, she looked across at him, dismissing any signs of resemblance.

After a long night, Lizzie's grandmother was discharged from the hospital and told to expose her heart to as little stress as possible. Back at the farm, Lizzie watched her grandfather wrap his arm around her grandmother as he carefully led her into the house. Last to enter was Lizzie's mother. There was something unusual about the way she stepped through the door. It was without hesitation.

Lizzie felt like screaming. She didn't like the way her grandfather helped her grandmother onto the sofa, so delicately, so convincingly. How could they act so normal around this man, when he had done something so horrific? Lizzie's mother marched towards the kitchen. 'Let's all have a cuppa,' she said. She lifted the fallen painting and hung it in its original place.

'Ah, who'd have thought I'd end up marrying the girl in red, eh?' Lizzie's grandfather asked, reaching out for his wife's hand. 'Mind you, that was many years after I painted her.' Lizzie looked at him, perplexed. He'd painted her? She'd thought the love of her grandmother's life had done that painting.

Lizzie's grandmother turned towards her daughter, who was now sitting on the armchair opposite. 'I'm really sorry, Alison, for blurting it all out to Lizzie. It's just, that painting, the girl, you know—'

141

'Don't be silly, Mum, it's fine. Look, we thought we'd lost you last night. That's all we were worried about. Clearly, nothing good comes from keeping secrets.'

'But Alison, I was such a fussy mother, needing to know of your whereabouts every minute of every day. And this man,' she pointed to Lizzie's grandfather, 'sometimes thought that because he wasn't, you know, your real dad—'

'Look, you've both always been perfect, you know that. We just have to make sure we do it right with Lizzie this time. No repeats!'

Lizzie looked at the large hand resting on her grandmother's shoulder and she felt her eyes relaxing, less focused than before. She went over to the sofa, circled her arms around her grandfather, laid her head on his shoulder and closed her eyes, breathing in the smell of hay and damp wool, which had over the years, sunk as deeply into his skin as it had into the walls of the farmhouse.

She drifted away as they talked. She moved along the carpet, towards the kitchen tiles and focused again, directly on the painting. As soon as she saw the familiar green and then the white of the farmhouse, it was obvious that the familiar face had disappeared. Lizzie wanted to scratch away at those layers to find the girl; she began to imagine her suffocating somewhere, hidden away where no rambler would be able to find her, buried beneath the house or the green of the fields. She waited and waited for the girl to reappear but the painting remained still.

Then, there she was. The girl in red was tiptoeing across the fields, as wary as ever, but managing a smile over her shoulder. Unaware, Lizzie's family talked and laughed in the next room, long strings of their sentences overlapping the next, and then the next. Lizzie noticed the front door of the farmhouse was ajar and the girl in red was stepping inside. Seconds later, she could see her chalky face looking through the window of the room above the icy pantry. There, caught behind the glass, was a red, little dress and a white, little hand pressing lightly against it. The girl's other hand, Lizzie imagined, was as always, clasping tightly onto her basket as though it cradled the world.

Belongings

A dozen white, plastic bags are planted around the office, containing belongings of the dead: a gold chain; inside-out knickers and an odd sock; lipstick worn down to the quick; glasses with a missing lens; pyjamas with the knees in. I see her name, written in black, permanent marker pen.

'They're hers,' I say, lifting the hollow bag from beside dusty stationery, unrolling the top. Inside, only sits a skinny watch, its leather strap cracking into hinges. The buckle, still fastened, points a silver finger as I try not to break its arms. The face is no longer ticking.

Acknowledgements

The book's epigraph is taken from Charlotte Perkins Gilman's *The Living of Charlotte Perkins Gilman* (New York: D. Appleton-Century Company, 1935), while the Oxford Dictionary definitions of waste used in 'Diary of a Waste Land' are those found on www.oxforddictionaries.com (accessed July 03, 2014).

A big thank you to Susie Wild for being a wonderful editor, to Richard Davies, Claire Houguez and everyone else at Parthian who has helped to create *Second-hand Rain*. Thank you to the ongoing support from Aida Birch, Alan & Jean Perry, organisers of The Terry Hetherington Award for featuring earlier versions of 'Lyrebird Lament' and 'Turnstones' in the 2012 and 2014 *Cheval* anthologies. Similarly, thank you to *Wales Arts Review* for commissioning 'Swansea Malady' for their fictional map of Wales series in 2013, and to Candy Jar Books for publishing an earlier version of 'Beautifully Greek' in *The Countess and the Mole Man* anthology. 'The Bereaved' first appeared in Parthian's *Rarebit: New Welsh Fiction,* an anthology of many, great writers whom it's been a pleasure to read alongside. A gigantic thank you to the assiduous Jon Gower for being such an encouraging mentor and for having faith in my stories from the beginning. A massive thank you to my always supportive and kind PhD supervisor, Stevie Davies, and I'd of course like to acknowledge the recently passed, much-loved and admired Nigel Jenkins, who supported my writing since the BA at Swansea. Thanks to everyone I've met through the English Department at Swansea

University (both students and lecturers) as well as everyone I've grown to know through the previously named The Crunch at *Mozarts*, since 2008, and the now-named Howl. Thank you to the good friends who attended my very first readings, and lastly, my biggest, biggest thanks of all go to my family, for understanding how important this first book is to me. I couldn't possibly have more support from you if I tried.

PARTHIAN

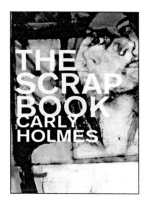

Three women, three generations: one dark secret...

A novel about the tangled, often dysfunctional, bonds of family; about soothing yourself with fairytales instead of challenging yourself to live with reality.

"Mysterious, esoteric and compassionate..." *Buzz Magazine*

"One of the most distinctive and exciting volumes of poetry to have come out of Wales in many years..." Jonathan Edwards

The Undressed is a poetry collection inspired by a cache of antique nude photographs of women. Meet Olive, the silent movie star, Karolina, 'The Folding Girl of Kotka', and Mary, the prostitute who hopes the judge she's due to stand before will turn out to be a client...

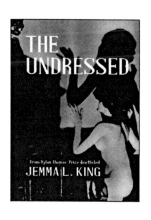

The sea's ghosts are stirring...

Pearl is haunted by the memory of lost love Nicholas. In this novel, steeped in the coast and people of Cornwall, the past can be more alive than the present...

"An evocative record of a lost age... unmistakably heartfelt." *Daily Mail*

NEW WRITING
www.parthianbooks.com

Lightning Source UK Ltd.
Milton Keynes UK
UKOW03f1237120914

238425UK00002B/19/P